Jake stepped around the open driver's side door and slid into the seat.

He turned the key. Only a clicking noise in response. Battery or alternator? He wasn't sure. Or maybe it was the starter.

"Do you think it's the battery?" She bit her lip. "That would be an easy fix."

"I don't think so. Can your mom or dad give you a ride home?"

She fixed a glare on him then softened her features. "My parents live in California. I think that would be a bit of a stretch for them to tote me home."

"Oh." He studied her face a little more closely. "Sorry, you almost look young enough to be a student. I thought you might be here for late summer registration."

"Ha! So what *grade* do you think I'm in?" She blinked, showing him a sassy grin. When he first arrived, he thought she'd been ready to crumble and fall into a pool of tears. Thankfully, she hadn't, although it was touch and go at first.

"A senior, of course." He cleared his throat. "So, you can't be old enough to be a parent of a high schooler, either. You must be a teacher."

She nodded. "Just moved to Starlight. I'm coaching color guard."

LYNETTE SOWELL is an award-winning author with New England roots, but she makes her home in central Texas with her husband and a herd of five cats. When she's not writing, she edits medical reports and chases down stories for the local newspaper. You can find out more about Lynette at lynettesowell.com, or find her on Facebook.

Counting on Starlight

Lynette Sowell

Heartsong Presents

For my Hannah-Banana—with memories of color guard, and one broken window.

A note from the Author:
I love to hear from my readers! You may correspond with me by writing:

Lynette Sowell
Author Relations
P.O. Box 9048
Buffalo, NY 14240-9048

ISBN-13: 978-0-373-48601-4

COUNTING ON STARLIGHT

This edition issued by special arrangement with Barbour Publishing, Inc., 1810 Barbour Drive, Uhrichsville, Ohio, U.S.A.

Scripture taken from the Holy Bible, New International Version®. NIV®. Copyright © 1973, 1978, 1984, 2011 by Biblica, Inc.™ Used by permission. All rights reserved worldwide.

one

In their hearts humans plan their course,
but the Lord establishes their steps.
PROVERBS 16:9

Liann Rivers gathered up the silk flag, saber, and wooden rifle then opened the door to the blast furnace outside the high school gymnasium. Late July in Texas never felt this hot when she visited Aunt Chin Mae and Uncle Bert way back when. However, during those days she'd done more wading in the Lampasas River and cruising around Belton Lake on Uncle Bert's boat than trudging across asphalt parking lots.

"See you on Monday morning," she called over her shoulder. Four days. That's all the time she had to listen to the CD in her purse and choreograph a routine for the Starlight High School marching band's flag team.

She crossed the parking lot and squinted at the figures over at the football practice field. The Starlight Yellowjackets—varsity football hopefuls, the band director told her. Here she was, in football country. Ironic that the athletic department could afford a full staff working with the team, even though the Human Resources director had talked to her about the district's budget cutbacks. She gritted her teeth. But she'd walked into the job here, eyes completely open. Almost.

Footsteps behind her on the asphalt made her turn around. It was Jessica, the band director, jogging in her direction and carrying a yellow lump of fabric.

"I forgot—here's your Yellowjackets spirit shirt." Jessica stopped and held up a shirt to Liann.

"My spirit shirt?" She could unfold it, but then she'd drop her equipment. She managed to pinch it between her fingers. Yellow was *not* her color.

"For Yellowjackets Spirit Day on Fridays." Jessica nodded solemnly as she wiped her brow with the back of her hand. "Every Friday during football season, we wear our Yellowjackets shirts to support the team."

Oh yes, the team. As if football players' and coaches' egos needed the support. Texas high school football was part of the religion in every town during the fall. Mere teachers didn't qualify for the sacred distinction.

She put on a smile. "I'll remember that. Thanks."

Jessica smiled. "I'm glad you're with us. It's a blessing in disguise, really. The district was ready to pull the color guard program from band, but I couldn't let them do that. I begged them to give us one more year. You were the perfect applicant for the job. I know you'll be able to push the girls to a higher level, especially with your cheer and gymnastics experience."

How could she respond to Jessica without revealing her swirling emotions? "I'm glad you think so. If anything, I've always been a fan of the underdog."

"Well, we have a whole slew of them for you, then." Jessica glanced toward the gymnasium. "Plus, the band could compete in UIL marching competitions, but without our color guard it's not as visually dramatic or beautiful. So we're counting on you. See you next week!" She turned and jogged back in the direction she came.

No pressure, of course. Liann shook her head and continued.

She had people counting on her to make something beautiful and graceful out of a lost cause. They had no idea what had brought her here, none at all. She could relate to lost causes.

Liann stopped at Trixie, her little red 1965 T-bird that made it all the way from California to Texas with only a flat tire. Right now she wanted to kick one of those tires. Instead, she opened her trunk and dumped the gear she carried, along with the T-shirt. She did allow herself to slam the trunk shut. Trixie groaned at the gesture.

"Lord, I knew this whole fiasco was a possibility, but I thought things would be better here." Liann bit her lip as she rounded the bumper and opened the car door. Even with the windows partly open, a fresh wave of heat radiated from inside the vehicle. She'd only been in the gymnasium for an hour to see her office, meet Starlight's band director, and discuss practice schedules, the fall football games, and marching competitions in October.

Some office, too. While gushing an apology, Jessica had shown Liann a corner of the supply room next to her office. Liann should have run screaming to the Starlight Independent School District administration office and shredded her offered teaching contract right then and there. But it was too late. She was here for the school year and might as well tuck herself into the bed she'd made for herself.

Ms. Rivers, I'm afraid we're only able to offer you a half-time position for this school year. Budget cutbacks, you understand, the director of Human Resources had said that morning. Half-time. She'd moved halfway across the country for a *half-time* position. Not as cheerleading coach either, for the Starlight squad. With her résumé, she figured she'd get the plum position.

We can use you as our color guard coach, since we're rebuilding the team. And she thought she'd left her color guard days behind her forever.

Liann stuck the key in Trixie's ignition. Staying in California was not an option. All doors had closed there, and she needed to put as much distance as she could between herself and Matt. It was better for everyone that way. She missed her parents. But Aunt Chin Mae and Uncle Bert had offered her their guest apartment over the garage when they learned she'd been offered a position in Starlight. Everything seemed like an answer to prayer. Until today, when all her plans came crashing down as soon as she'd arrived in Starlight's main administration office.

Liann turned the key and only heard clicking instead of the engine turning over. "No, no, no. . ." She turned the key again with the same response.

Great. Now she *would* kick her car. Uncle Bert was fishing and probably had his phone turned off so he could have some peace and quiet. Or so he said. Aunt Chin Mae was at the nail salon working, so that left her. . .stranded for the moment. "Lord, I sure could use a hand."

❧

Jake Tucker squinted across the practice field and at the parking lot. The slim figure of a young woman popped the hood of a flaming-red ancient T-bird. He dragged his attention back to the boys on the field, performing defensive drills. He and the coaching team had an entire defensive roster to sort through, and by the end of July some guys would be elated while others would prepare to warm their hind ends on the bench.

That was the way it went with football. Either you had it, or you didn't. A few of the scrappier guys would grow as players from their freshman year onward, but four years wasn't a long time to build on playing skills.

He glanced at his watch. They'd been at it for thirty minutes now. Time for a break. Nobody needed heat exhaustion—or worse—from working on drills in these temperatures. He was just standing there and his golden yellow polo shirt clung to his chest and back. Coach Blann was inside at his desk going through his playbook. He'd been relying on Jake more during the summer practice season, it seemed. Jake wondered if the man had health issues. But Blann never volunteered information, and Jake didn't ask.

"Take ten minutes, guys," he shouted through his cupped hands. "Get some water and get some shade." He glanced across the parking lot again. Now the figure had her hands propped on her hips, still staring at the car's engine.

He might as well see if he could help. He knew something about cars. Not as much as he did about football, but enough. Heat shimmered from the parking lot.

"Hi there," he called out to the young lady at the red car. "What seems to be the trouble?"

"Trixie." She frowned at the vehicle and pulled her ink-black hair away from her neck, fanning herself. Her dark eyes had just a hint of an exotic tilt at the corners.

"Does it turn over, Trixie?"

"Oh, *she's* Trixie." The young woman pointed at the car. "No, she won't turn over. I have no idea what's wrong. I mean, she's been making this rattling noise lately, but I figured it was because of the long road trip." Her voice caught.

"I see. . . . I'm Coach Tucker, by the way."

"It would be nice to meet you, under better circumstances." She swallowed and placed her hand on her forehead. "I have no idea why she chose now to quit. Better than on the road or in the middle of nowhere, but this just caps off my day perfectly. Never mind. . ." She shook her head.

"Let me see what I can do." Jake stepped around the open driver's side door and slid into the seat. He turned the key. Only a clicking noise in response. Battery or alternator? He wasn't sure. Or maybe it was the starter.

"Do you think it's the battery?" She bit her lip. "That would be an easy fix."

"I don't think so. Can your mom or dad give you a ride home?"

She fixed a glare on him then softened her features. "My parents live in California. I think that would be a bit of a stretch for them to tote me home."

"Oh." He studied her face a little more closely. "Sorry, you almost look young enough to be a student. I thought you might be here for late summer registration."

"Ha! So what *grade* do you think I'm in?" She blinked, showing him a sassy grin. When he first arrived, he thought she'd been ready to crumble and fall into a pool of tears. Thankfully, she hadn't, although it was touch and go at first.

"A senior, of course." He cleared his throat. "So, you can't be old enough to be a parent of a high schooler, either. You must be a teacher."

She nodded. "Just moved to Starlight. I'm coaching color guard."

"Good luck on that one."

"What's wrong with the color guard?"

"They have nowhere else to go but up. If they don't improve this year, the school board is prepared to shut down the program."

"Is that right?" She propped her hands on her hips once again.

"I'm just tellin' you what I heard." He had a feeling that when she heard challenges like that, she'd try to prove someone wrong. He liked that. She had a winner's mentality. Plus a playful grin that even now melted into a scowl at her car.

"Well, I'm not going to whip anyone into shape if I'm stuck here. My aunt's at work and my uncle's out fishing. I don't know a soul in town."

"You know me."

"Ha. Hardly. But, do you know of a good towing service? I don't have Triple-A anymore." She shook her head. "I guess I should be thankful I didn't break down like this during the move."

"I can call Herb Bush. Retired army, has a tow truck for hire, and he'll take Trixie anywhere you like. Even the junkyard." He couldn't resist teasing her, just to see the spark in her eyes.

"Not hardly. She's a '65 T-bird. But seriously, if you could give me his number, I'll call him myself." She gestured with her head toward the practice field. "I think your team is ready to get practicing again. Either that, or they're trying really hard to hear what we're talking about."

Jake glanced over his shoulder. The squad of varsity hopefuls lined up along the chain-link fence that separated the practice field from the parking lot. Great. Now he'd hear the guys ribbing him when he returned. Just let 'em try it.

He pulled out his cell phone and called Aunt Zalea. "Hey, Aunt Zalea. . .it's Jake. Is Uncle Herb around? Someone at the high school is broken down, needs a tow."

"Hey, honey. He's just sittin' here, staring at the back of his eyeballs, letting the ice melt in his sweet tea." Aunt Zalea's drawl crossed the phone line. Jake could just make out mumbling in the background, something about not taking a nap, just reading a book. "Well, Herb, you've been on that same page for thirty minutes now. Okay, Jake. He'll be there in about fifteen minutes."

Jake ended the call. "Herb's on his way. If you take her anywhere, don't go to Starlight Auto. Go to Biff's."

"Biff's?"

"Yup. They'll do right by you, and Trixie." Biff Hutchins and Jake went way back, from their first days in a new high school after their fathers were both transferred to nearby Fort Hood at the same time. Jake had done the college thing, Biff had gone the trades route.

"Wow, thanks for the tip. And for your help." She smiled at him. Her smile didn't quite reach her eyes.

"Hey, Coach!" A voice drifted across the parking lot. Tim Rollins, who'd likely end up as starting quarterback if he kept up his passing and running.

"I'll be right there," Jake hollered back. Oh yeah, he'd hear about it all right. "You take care. Do you need any water or anything? It gets really hot on this parking lot."

"I'll be fine. And thanks, I appreciate it. Now go, before those boys really start harassing you." She waved him off.

Jake trotted back to the practice field. He stepped onto the curb and realized something: he didn't know the young mystery woman's name. One thing was for sure: he was glad it *wasn't* Trixie.

two

"Me 'n' Zalea and the Riverses have been friends for years, just so you know. Me 'n' Bert were in Nam together, got out of the army around '85 or so, but Starlight just wouldn't let any of us go. So, here we are," Herb Bush said as they roared along out of town a mile or so to the Rivers farm. He'd towed Trixie right over to Biff's then offered to drive Liann to her aunt and uncle's.

"I see. I used to visit here in the summer sometimes. My mom and Chin Mae are sisters." Liann watched the barbed-wire fences whip past, with gnarled live oak trees dotting the pasture land.

"Oh, so *you're* Nam Sun's daughter. Chin told us they were gettin' the spare room all set up." He gave Liann a sideways look. "That Jake Tucker's a fine young man. Glad he called me to help ya."

Yes, Jake Tucker was pretty fine, but she wasn't looking. Way too soon for her to even search for the word *romance* in the dictionary. "I'm glad he did, too. So how much do I owe you for the tow?"

Herb downshifted and turned into the driveway, where a sign proclaimed RIVERS HONEY with a graphic of a beehive. "Nothin'. You're family. Your uncle's like a brother to me. B'sides, nobody should break down on their first day in Starlight."

Breaking down, her first day in Starlight. Liann had to grin at his statement. Forget about Trixie. Herb Bush had *no* idea how close she'd come to crying a river of tears and watching them evaporate on the parking lot.

Her aunt's car, a tiny Smart Car in metallic gold, sparkled in the driveway, and Herb stopped behind it. "Well, thanks, Mr. Bush."

"Uncle Herb. I'm Uncle Herb to everyone in Starlight."

She nodded. "Okay. And be sure to thank Jake Tucker for me."

"Will do. Biff'll do right by your little Trixie. You'll see."

Liann climbed down from the truck's cab and waved as Herb drove off. She could have called Aunt Chin Mae, although she couldn't imagine herself stuffed into her aunt's car, winding their way out of town back to the farm.

She ambled along to the house, glancing to her left and out at the rippling fields with beehives tucked underneath the oak trees. Rivers Honey had turned from a retirement hobby into a full-time venture. She'd stay away from the hives, thank you very much. The very thought of the tens of thousands of bees in each hive made Liann shiver as she took the first step to her apartment over the garage.

As soon as she entered the cool one-room efficiency, she slapped her forehead. She'd left all the equipment and that hideous yellow shirt in Trixie's trunk. Liann found a gallon of sweet tea in the small refrigerator, which Aunt Chin Mae had stocked with all kinds of beverages. She pushed it aside and instead reached for a bottle of tropical fruit juice.

She sank onto the love seat and watched the ceiling fan do its thing of circulating the cool air. What she really needed was some girlfriend chat. Beth, her best friend, still considered her move to Texas a crazy one. But Beth loved her enough to know Liann needed to go, given the circumstances. Liann looked at her phone. It was nearly one o'clock, which made it eleven in California. She dialed Beth's number.

"Hey you! I'm surprised to hear from you. I figured it would be at least a week until you got settled into your routine." Beth's voice reminded her of all the good things she'd left behind. Her parents, special friends, a great church, an excellent job—maybe Beth was right. . . .

"I just needed to hear a friendly voice." Liann tried to control the quaver in her words.

"What's wrong?"

"Everything. I'm not coaching cheer. I'm coaching the color guard. It's a half-time position. Do you know what that means? I moved over one thousand miles for a part-time job. I was sure I'd get the cheer position. Maybe not one hundred percent sure, but. . .you know I had to come. . ."

"How can they do that? From cheer to color guard?"

Liann explained, and capped off her whole sorry morning by saying, "and Trixie broke down and she had to be towed. I don't know how I'm going to be able to afford repairs. My savings are slim, and I don't get paid until August fifteenth."

"Oh, girl. I knew it was a bad idea to totally start over in such a drastic way. . . . Not a bad idea to dump Matt, though."

Liann pondered her disappointments for a moment. "Still, the tow-truck guy is good friends with my uncle and didn't charge me, and the coach I met told me I should send Trixie to his friend who owns an auto repair shop and won't overcharge me."

"You know you could have moved in with me. I don't mind having a roommate, considering you'd broken your lease."

"I know, and I appreciate it. But Matt—"

"Matt's going to survive."

"I know he will. But he never listened to me, and I doubt he'd start now. Which is why Starlight seemed a better option. I need the distance."

Beth filled her in on everything she'd missed in the five days since she'd left La Vida, California. She'd returned the last of the gifts that Liann had received at the bridal shower, and Liann didn't have to face any of the unspoken questions about why she'd made her big decision. Life had gone on without her. Even Beth hurried off the phone with a promise to keep in touch.

❧

"We had registration today," Madelynn Tucker announced at supper that evening. She glanced at Jake then down at her dinner plate.

Jake looked up from his notepad next to his plate of chicken-fried steak. Sixteen-year-old Maddie sure could cook, but comfort food during the week in the summertime meant something was up. "I thought you were already registered for classes."

"Well, um, I am." Maddie stepped into the kitchen. "Want some more sweet tea? I'm almost out."

"No, I'm good." If it wasn't because of Dad's health problems, Mom and Dad would still be here in Starlight. The idea of watching over his sister for the last few years of high school after his parents moved to Colorado last year had been easy to agree to. Maddie was smart, a good kid, generally listened to him and Billy, and they kept in touch with their parents via weekly Skype meetings. Ever since his younger brother Billy had married Justine Campbell in June, they'd been busy setting up house, working on the new buildings for the soldiers' retreat on the Tucker farm, and well, being newlyweds.

Jake didn't mind keeping an eye on Maddie. She didn't even turn the other way when they saw each other in the halls, and she wore her brother's football coach status as her own badge of honor.

Maddie returned with a plastic pitcher and poured herself a fresh glass of tea. "Today was the last day to make schedule changes before school starts, so I did."

"Ah, I see. You talked to Mom and Dad, I assume?"

"Yup. They said it was fine, once I explained."

"Well, we're going to start the new practice schedule soon. You ready?"

"Um, here's the thing. . . . I'm not going to be a trainer anymore." Maddie straightened her posture. "I changed my schedule, like I said."

"What are you talking about?" Jake shook his head. "You've got a great résumé built up. If you're going to UT for premed it'll look good that you've got four years as a trainer."

Maddie shrugged. "I don't think I want to do premed anymore. That's a lot of school. I know I'm a junior, but I've made my mind up."

"You sure you talked to Mom and Dad?" Unbelievable. All she'd talked about since junior high was one day becoming a physician. She wanted to treat families and open a practice here in Starlight after she finished her residency.

"Yes. They said it was fine. I don't see why this is a big deal." She took a sip of her tea.

Of course she didn't. She was sixteen and was already an expert on life. Jake frowned. "So what are you planning to do now?"

"I dunno. I decided to take home ec, for one thing. I like cooking, a lot. And I need another PE credit, so I signed up for color guard since they had plenty of room in that class." Now her shoulders drooped. "You're mad."

"No, I'm not mad." Jake paused a moment. Teenagers' emotions flared up one moment then deflated the next. He needed to choose his words carefully. "I'm shocked, for one thing, that you didn't tell me sooner. And I'm disappointed. I really enjoyed having you along with the team when we traveled."

"That's why I didn't say anything." Maddie sighed. "I knew you'd be upset. I didn't do it to hurt your feelings. I'm real proud that you're my brother, but I wanted to do something. . . different."

"I'll say. Color guard is miles away from being a trainer." Plus, he didn't dare add that Maddie had the coordination of a rhinoceros trying to roller-skate. "Now, cooking. That I can see you excelling in."

She nodded. "I can't wait. Plus, I signed up for the dual credit option with the college, the intro to culinary arts course. Dad faxed the permission slip to the counselor."

Wow. They'd been cooking this one up for some time—no pun intended—and he'd missed it. "I guess you've got it all figured out."

"Yup." Maddie grinned as she scooped up a bite of mashed potatoes with her fork. "Thanks for understanding, Jake. You're the best."

"Please, Maddie. I know I'm not our dad, but if you're ever having a hard time making a decision, come talk to me. That's what I'm here for." He wondered how long she would last in color guard. The marching band worked just as hard at their drills as the football team did, mirroring the team's twelve-hour practice schedules during the first week of August. Mom and Dad were far away, and they had no idea that Maddie was actually lowering her potential. Color guard, on a premed student's application? She might be accepted to the college because of her grades, but that didn't mean she'd be accepted into the premed program.

Of course, he'd just met the new color guard instructor in the parking lot today. He knew just where to find her, too. If Maddie started to crash and burn with this latest change of plans, he'd go straight to the new teacher and see if she could persuade Maddie to change her classes back to her old schedule.

He wouldn't mind seeing that teacher again. He liked her spunk, her drive. She needed a truckload of it to take on the faltering color guard team. He spent halftimes in the locker room, but even there, the dismal tales of the marching band's color guard squad filtered back to him and the rest of the coaching staff. Her brave smile told him she was up to the challenge. He had a feeling she might be able to handle the changing whims of a teenager just fine.

&

Liann felt like she was breathing through a collapsed straw. Heat prickled down her back and along both of her arms, covered in long sleeves and leather-palmed gloves that went up to her forearms. She thought she'd get her mind out of today's doldrums by helping her aunt with the bees. She tried to tamp down her fears. Her efforts weren't working so well—the perspiration all over her body wasn't only from the blistering sun. She cleared her throat to hide the tremor in her voice. "How—how many bees did you say were in this hive?"

"Fifty thousand." Aunt Chin Mae lifted the top box from the beehive. "Here. Smoke the bottom again."

Liann pressed the tiny bellows on the smoker, and puffs of smoke came from the spout, swirling down to the box. "I can't believe I'm doing this."

"We move slow and take our time. Today, I clean the brood boxes and you fill the feeders." She removed the next hive. "So, you have a bad day?"

"Oh, Aunt Chin Mae. . ." Liann squeezed the bellows again. "I'm so happy you and Uncle Bert are letting me stay here, but. . .it's been a hard day."

"God has a plan, Li."

"It's not that simple."

"So when things are going your way, you can see His plan? Does His plan mean we always get our way, like a two-year-old?" Aunt Chin Mae straightened, propping one hand on her hip.

"No. But I'm not acting like a two-year-old."

"You made a big decision to leave California, all because you do not know your own mind."

Liann hung her head. "I couldn't marry Matt. I couldn't. I should have—"

"I know. You should have called it off before you sent out the invitations." Her aunt hissed, shaking her head. "All that money you spent. . .and you did not know you didn't love him?"

"I did care for him, *loved* him. The wedding got so. . .big. I don't know." She watched Aunt Chin Mae lift the top from the box. "I couldn't think, I couldn't breathe. . . ." Like now. Thousands of honeybees swirled and pulsed on the frames inside the hive, turning themselves into a mass that thought and moved as one.

"You ran away." Her aunt waved her closer. "Empty the feeder and refill it."

Liann turned away and lugged the five-gallon bucket full of honeybee food closer to the hive. "I didn't run away. I called off the wedding and figured I needed a fresh start." She pulled out the plastic feeder and dumped the leftover liquid, along with a few dead bees, at the foot of the nearest oak tree. When she returned, she filled the feeder with fresh food and returned it to the hive.

"You a runaway bride." Aunt Chin Mae shrugged. "It happens. You take a time-out and see what God wants for you."

They restacked the hive and moved on to the next hive under a nearby tree. This was crazy. She was inches away from groups of bees who could swarm around her, crawl under the cuffs of her sleeves, and. . . No wonder she ran from California. "How do I know what God wants for me? I hardly know what I want for myself."

"You young people think too hard. You go off and do things without listening."

"Listening?"

"You have elders in your life. God gives elders to help you. Your father, he did not want you to marry Matt. Said you were leaping too soon, too excited. You are in love with love." Her aunt repeated the process at this hive.

"I'm twenty-six, Aunt Chin Mae. I'm not a baby. I know how to make decisions." Her own words rang in her ears. She'd just said she didn't know what she wanted for herself. "Dad never said anything to me about him not really wanting me to marry Matt." Not really. Although Liann had to admit she never quite asked. She simply did what she thought was best at the time.

"Your father tried to talk to you, but you don't know how to listen. A wise person listens to counselors. A fool ignores good advice."

"That sounds like something out of Proverbs." She couldn't help but smile at her aunt's intensity and her own fumbling.

"It is." Aunt Chin Mae waited as Liann filled the bee feeder. "There. And see, God has been taking care of you. He provided a way home for you today. Your car is taken care of. Good thing Jake Tucker saw you having trouble."

"True, but if he hadn't come, I would have gone back into the school."

"Yes, but God presented your solution before you even had a problem."

Liann sighed. It couldn't be that simple. She didn't believe in just letting things happen to you. If people thought that, then people would never step out, take chances.

Jake Tucker. He reminded her of why she left California, left Matt. He was confident, take-charge, sure of himself in a way that was nothing short of charming. . .things that had drawn her to Matt in the first place. One easy decision for her, though. She wouldn't get herself entangled while here in Starlight. She didn't need the complication, didn't know how long she'd be here. Plus, she wouldn't let herself get sucked in to more ideas with someone with a strong personality.

three

The winding road had a generous amount of shoulder as Liann jogged along, enjoying the morning breeze. Another scorcher coming, but she was determined to beat the heat and get her three miles in. She didn't want last night's blue mood to follow her into a new day.

This morning she'd read in Proverbs, the book of Wisdom. She needed wisdom not to make the same mistakes twice. Plus, last night she'd checked her e-mail. Matt had sent three in the last week, the most recent one from yesterday. Ironically, it arrived around the same time she'd been stranded at the school.

Li, I don't understand what it is that I've done wrong. Call me. We can work it out. Even if all we do is go to a justice of the peace, I still want to marry you. Our plane tickets are still good for Wyoming, and we can still reserve a cabin.

He really thought she'd change her mind if he held on long enough. He just didn't get it. It didn't come down to the wedding, even though the menu only had one thing on it that she liked, even though the guest list had mushroomed to nearly two hundred. She almost stopped short on the road.

She didn't want to go camping at Yellowstone for her honeymoon, not even in a cabin with electricity and running water. She really wanted to go to the Caribbean, find a quiet patch of beach, and watch the sun rise every morning. And go horseback riding, snorkeling, maybe investigate the culture of the island.

Then why hadn't she ever told Matt? Why not, indeed? "Poor Matt," she knew people were saying back home. She hadn't lied to him, ever. But she'd buried herself and gone along with him.

Liann quickened her pace, dug in to climb the slight incline, and let herself grin when she reached the top. These Texas roads were steeper than they looked and could fool a runner until they were already heading up the grade. She refused to let her burning legs make her stop.

Sweat burned her eyes. Next time, she'd bring a headband or something to keep herself from running off the road while wiping her eyes. Another figure, a man, was jogging in her direction. Something about his shoulders and posture told her she'd seen him before. Jake, the football coach.

He snapped to attention and looked straight in her direction. He waved first then crossed over the road to meet her.

"G'morning." His arms bore a sheen of sweat, as did his face and neck.

"Hey there. Trying to beat the heat?" she asked.

"Yes. I don't think it worked." He fell into step beside her. "Mind if I run with you for a few minutes?"

Part of her wanted to turn round and run home. But a car drove by, and its driver honked and waved.

"Hey, Coach," a teenage boy called out the driver's window. "Getting your miles in early?"

"Yes, trying to," said Jake. "See you at nine?"

"Sure thing." With that, the young man sped off.

"That's Tim. He's a good kid. He'll likely make starting

quarterback." Jake glanced at her. "You okay? This heat can sure sap your energy and dry you out quickly."

"I'm managing. I thought I came out early enough before the heat was bad, but I guess not." She tried not to puff as she jogged along. Jake had to shorten his stride for her to keep up with him. He could probably beat her in sprints, no problem.

"So, how's Trixie?"

"I dunno. Biff never called. Either he was busy, or whatever's broken is worse than we thought."

"He'll call. He's thorough." They continued along, stride for stride. "So, Trixie's owner. What's your real name?"

"Liann Rivers."

"You know Bert and Chin Mae?"

"My aunt and uncle."

"We're almost neighbors." He nodded down the road. "Tucker Ranch."

"Ah, okay." She tried not to glance to the side. Jake Tucker had the physique of a running back and plenty of speed. He didn't run with his feet slapping the pavement, and he carried his weight well.

"Race me to the gate?"

"No, you'll beat me." She kept jogging, refusing to let him see any sign that her legs were in flames and the stitch in her side threatened to make her gasp.

"Are you so sure?"

"Of course. You're at least eight inches taller than me, for one thing." She glanced up at him. He had to be teasing her. "Plus you're holding back with your stride. And you can talk just fine. Me, on the other hand. . ." She tried not to pant and run at the same time.

"I could let you win." He chuckled.

Good grief. She hoped he could fit through the ranch gate ahead with the size of his head. She jogged a few more strides before speaking. "I don't need anyone to let me win."

"No, I guess you don't." He lengthened his stride. "Catch me if you can."

"Not today. See you around, Jake Tucker." She tried not to roll her eyes as the distance increased between them and he headed to the gate for Tucker Ranch. She did, however, stop along the side of the road after he passed through the gate. She leaned over and bent at the waist with her hands resting on her knees, gasping for air.

She might as well have been sitting in a sauna for half an hour, the way sweat poured from her arms and legs and ran down her back. Her pulse roared in her head. She sucked in a breath. Walk it out. She needed to walk it out. She fought to keep her feet moving, even plodding along, but they felt like she had bricks strapped to them.

"Hey, are you all right?" Jake stopped just inside the gate. He tilted to one side. Or maybe that was her.

"Just. . .need. . .to catch my breath." She tried to gulp more air. "I have a stitch." She sank onto the grassy roadside, hearing Jake call her name, sounding like he was at the end of a long tin can. Please, no snakes next to the road, or in the tall, dry grass just this side of the barbed-wire fence. Aunt Chin Mae told her never to go barefoot outside and to always watch out for snakes in the field.

Strong arms helped lift her up. "C'mon, you need to get cooled off."

"I'm fine, really. Just felt a little light-headed for a minute." Liann tried to pull away, but part of her didn't mind leaning on him as he helped her along the driveway. A long ranch house lay catty-corner to the end of the drive, and a small stone building lay at the other side of the driveway with a barn and a few other outbuildings behind them. This was how she'd gone through life, letting people and things pull her along. She'd given up her voice. Not anymore. She tried to pull away and stand on her own.

At that moment, she also realized the potential trap she'd stepped into. Jogging, alone, in an unfamiliar place. So what if Starlight wasn't the big city? She was letting a man she'd only met once—albeit as a Good Samaritan—take her down his driveway, to his home. She stopped her stumbling gait along the driveway.

Jake paused, and she allowed herself to meet his hazel eyes. "Look, it'll take a few minutes to get you cooled off and hydrated. My sister's in the house. She was a trainer for the football team, and she knows how to treat heat exhaustion." His arm around her waist loosened, but he continued to help her along.

"Sorry, thanks, but I'm going to walk back to my aunt's house."

"I don't think that's a good idea right now. You need cool compresses and electrolytes and some cool air. If you want to call your aunt or someone and tell them you're okay before you go inside, go ahead. I don't mind." He released her and pulled his cell phone from his belt. She stood there and tried not to sway.

She felt like she was talking around cotton in her mouth. "Okay." She took his phone and dialed.

"Who is this?" Aunt Chin Mae answered, skipping the typical hello as usual.

"It's Liann."

"Whose phone you using? Where are you? I thought you were running."

"I am. I don't feel well. I met up with Jake Tucker, and we're at the Tucker Ranch. I'm using Jake's phone."

"Okay. You need me to come get you?"

"No, no thanks. I'll see you soon." She glanced at Jake, who stood there with his arms folded. She ended the call and handed the phone back to Jake.

She didn't really need rescuing, and yet here was Jake Tucker again. But he'd stopped long enough to let her make a phone call. She clamped a hand on her stomach to stave off the wave of nausea that hit her.

"What's wrong?" Jake asked.

Liann shook her head. No way was she going to lose her coffee and muffin in front of him. She covered her mouth with one hand then leaned to the side and emptied her stomach on a poor unsuspecting cactus at the side of the driveway.

๛

Liann stood there, pale as a sheet of paper and swaying like a leaf. Jake wanted to carry her the rest of the way to the house, but she'd probably fly at him and accuse him of making a pass at her. He didn't dare look at the liquidy mess on the cactus.

"C'mon, we need to get you inside. I've seen this before. You're dehydrated." He allowed himself to place his hand on her shoulder.

Liann nodded. "I'm so sorry." She glanced over her shoulder as she hobbled along. "Do you have a garden hose handy? I can clean it up."

"Don't worry about it." He glanced at her, noting the sweat on her brow, on her arms. "Can you make it?"

She nodded. "I can do it."

He fought to keep his pace slow, but he'd seen people knocked on their backs by the heat. They drew closer to the house. Liann looked pale, but she'd set her jaw. Stubborn woman. Then her foot tripped on a rock.

Jake caught her from stumbling in time then kept his arm securely around her. "Almost there." She didn't pull away but looked up at him as she nodded. He saw strength in her dark eyes.

So far he'd made himself immune to the ladies of Starlight, many of whom seemed to like his title of assistant coach. In a year, though, Lord willing, Starlight would be behind him, and he'd be on to the next big thing. Maybe he'd make time for a relationship then. But not now. Some ladies thought they could deal with the life of being with a coach, but at least six months out of the year he worked fifteen-hour days, and it was all about the team. Most women wouldn't put up with that.

Onward and upward for him, even if it meant flying solo with whatever God brought him. But with one direct gaze from Liann, his forward momentum paused, just as Liann's footsteps had stumbled. Crazy. He'd only seen her twice, had known her name less than an hour. He didn't need a distraction like this. Like her.

The front door banged open. "What's wrong?" Maddie flew outside.

"Get some dishcloths. Run them under cool water. Grab some Gatorade, too—no ice," Jake called out. He whisked Liann inside, following his sister into the house.

"I can walk on my own now," Liann said, but she still leaned on him as they entered the kitchen. She sank onto the nearest dining chair. Maddie approached with the dishcloths.

"Thanks." He grabbed the cloths and pulled up another chair. "Here, put this one behind your neck."

She reached for the cloth, but Jake held it on her neck. With the other cloth, she wiped her face and arms.

"Here's more, for behind your knees." Maddie also placed a plastic cup of Gatorade next to Liann's elbow. Then she knelt in front of Liann. "We need to get your running shoes and socks off, too."

Liann's color was already coming back. "Wow, I don't know what happened to me back there. One minute I was fine, the next I was just ready to lie down. The air-conditioning feels great." She reached for the cup of Gatorade and took a sip.

"Don't sip too much," Maddie said as she took one of the other chairs. "Did you eat breakfast or hydrate this morning?"

"I had a muffin and half a cup of coffee." Liann swallowed more of the Gatorade. "You're right, Jake. I didn't hydrate."

Maddie shook her head. "That's disaster around here in the Texas heat." No wonder she'd wanted to be a doctor, was meant to be a doctor. Jake wished she'd realize how natural she was, even now, with a cool head and knowing exactly what to do.

"Liann, meet my sister, Madelynn," Jake said. "She's going to be a junior at Starlight High this year."

"Nice to meet you, Madelynn." Liann smiled. "I'm staying with my aunt and uncle down the road and met up with your brother while out for my run. I'm glad he was there when I got sick."

"Me, too." Jake took the cloth from behind Liann's neck, leaving her hair sticking to her skin. She looked pretty, even in her slightly frazzled state. "Maddie, Ms. Rivers is the new color guard coach."

"You *are*?" Maddie switched from trainer mode to teenage girl. "I can't *wait* to start! Jake had a cow last night when he found out I changed my schedule. But it's going to be great. My friend Shayla in the marching band said that the music is from *Beauty and the Beast* this year, too. I can't wait to see our uniforms. How long have you done color guard?"

Liann blinked at Maddie's nonstop chatter then laughed. "I used to be a cheer coach, but back in high school I performed in color guard for a while. I'm definitely going to count on your enthusiasm this season. It's going to be a relearning process for me, but we're going to have a great time. The music selections are terrific, very dramatic." Liann glanced at Jake.

Jake looked at his watch. "I need to go soon myself. Liann, what time do you need to be at the school?"

"Nine, at the latest. What time is it now?" She sat up straighter in her chair.

"Seven forty-five."

"Ack." Liann took another sip of the Gatorade. "I really should get back. I have a lot of planning to do."

"Well, you're not walking—or running—back to your aunt and uncle's house." Jake crossed his arms across his chest.

"Can I drive? Please? I need to practice before I can go for my road test." Maddie bounced on her toes then ran to get her car keys on the wall peg before Jake could answer.

"She really gets her mind made up, doesn't she?" Liann laughed.

"You have no idea." Jake hoped Liann was up to the challenge of channeling Maddie back to her true calling— being a physician. He didn't see what twirling a flag or tossing a saber had to do with that.

four

"Okay, ladies. It's four o'clock." Liann clapped her hands, and the troupe of eight girls collapsed onto the gymnasium floor, their flags fluttering to the ground after them. For the past week, she'd been working the girls through a simple routine. Several of them admitted they'd tried out for the cheerleading squad and didn't make it.

"If you can't do a backflip, you don't stand a chance of being a cheerleader," said Kristen, a lanky brunette. "I can do cartwheels, the splits, and high kicks all day long. But to them, I'm still a loser and got cut 'cause I can't do a backflip."

"Well, I can guarantee you we won't be working on back-flips here. And, you're not a loser." Liann swallowed hard. How many girls had she turned away from the cheer squad in California for the same reason? After dozens of hopefuls paraded through the gym, cheering and flipping and showing tons of team spirit, it was easy to dismiss those who didn't cut it or didn't have the gymnastics skills. She couldn't choose everyone. Plus, precision was everything in cheer.

She hoped she never made any of these girls feel less than the beautiful young women they were. Maddie was busy tying her sneaker. Now *that* girl had no coordination. She'd hit herself on the head with her own flag at last three times. When Liann had led the team left in time to the music, Maddie went to the right then corrected herself.

"All right, you have your CDs. You should have already

loaded the music to your MP3 player or phone or laptop or whatever. Listen to it every day. And this weekend, I want you to work on fifty spins in each direction. If you get brave, try a toss and catch." Liann started spinning her own practice flag, using one hand. She didn't tell them she'd spent the weekend reacquiring her old skills. "One word of warning: no spinning flags in the house. Windows aren't cheap to replace."

They giggled as they gathered their flags, picked up their CDs from the table beside the wall, and left. Maddie stayed behind.

"Ms. Rivers?" Maddie approached her, dragging her flag behind her. "You're not going to cut me, are you? Because I know I'm not that good. And just so you know, Jake doesn't want me to be in this class."

Liann unplugged the CD player and picked it up. "Of course I'm not going to cut you from the team. I assure you it's a challenge to learn spinning, and how to move in time with the others on the team and move with the music. But we'll practice so much that you will be able to walk through the routine blindfolded—without hurting yourself or anyone else. By October, I'll have you spinning a saber."

Maddie sighed, her shoulders relaxing. "Oh, that's good. There's something about the beautiful music and us moving the flags in time. I can feel the song. It's so joyful. Does that sound crazy?"

"No, not to me." Liann smiled. A memory flickered in the corner of her mind of a teenage girl with dark hair, leaving the color guard behind because she wanted to be "in." Once upon a time, she'd been content to spin her flag until taunts from someone else made her want to quit the team and leave her friends behind.

"You okay, Ms. Rivers?"

"I'm fine. I'm just thinking." She started toward her office with Maddie walking beside her. "Now, why doesn't Jake want you in this class?"

"He thinks it's going to hurt my college résumé."

"Really?" What was the deal with that guy? Liann flipped on her office light. "Why?"

"Since I'm a junior now, at this point I only need half a credit in PE to make the rest of my health and PE graduation requirements. Color guard is one and a half PE credits, plus half a music credit." Maddie caught the tip of her flag on the top of the doorway, the pole striking her forehead. "Ow!"

"Maddie, are you okay?" Liann almost felt the crack of wood on her own head. "Careful with doorways."

"I'm okay." Maddie rubbed her forehead and lowered the tip of the flag. "But Jake thinks I need to change my schedule back and be a trainer for the football team."

"Did you talk to your parents about it?" Liann wasn't sure she wanted to get involved in the middle of a family controversy, but she really liked this kid and her enthusiasm. Maybe Maddie wouldn't be the most proficient at color guard, yet no one could doubt her dedication to doing a good job. Liann suspected that trait ran in the Tucker family.

"I did. Mom and Dad said it was fine. They didn't mind."

"But Jake?" Liann knew his type. Push until you got your way, push across the forty-yard line until you got the first down.

"I was going to be a doctor someday." Maddie sank onto the nearest plastic chair. "Even since junior high, I worked with the football team as a trainer. If one of the guys sprained an ankle or jammed a finger, I was there. Or if someone got sick or knocked on the head, I was there."

"So that explains you being so efficient when I was sick from the heat the other morning."

"I just know what to do. I love being with my brother. I'm so proud of him. But I can't breathe. I feel like he's always watching." Maddie sighed and rolled her eyes.

Spoken like a typical teenager. "I see. Well, he's your brother and he loves you. He's responsible for you."

"Well, it's not like he's going to cut my food up for me. But it feels that way."

"Do you still want to be a doctor? I'm sure he's thinking ahead to you getting into college. It's very competitive."

"I'm in the top ten percent of my class. If you graduate in the top ten percent in Texas, you get admission to any Texas public university."

"Wow, it sounds like you've done your homework. So, what about you becoming a doctor?"

"I. . .I'm not sure. I like helping people. I'm good at math and science. But the idea of having everything so planned out for my life right now. . ."

"Maybe he'll come around in time, when he sees how much you're enjoying color guard."

Maddie shrugged. "He's pretty stubborn. But you can't cut me. I'm going to do a great job. You'll see."

"I'm sure you'll make great improvements. You're determined, and that's half the battle sometimes." Liann wasn't sure how much Maddie would improve, but she didn't have the heart to discourage the girl. And part of her really wanted Maddie to prove Jake wrong.

A figure appeared in the doorway behind Maddie. Kristen,

from the squad. "Hey, excuse me. Maddie, someone's waiting for you outside."

Maddie ran her hand over her hair. "Really? Who?"

"You know. . . ." Kristen half leaned in the doorway, her gaze flicking over to Liann. "Remember. . .Tim?"

"Oh, that's right." Maddie leaped to her feet. "Thanks, Ms. Rivers, for listening. I can't wait till we see our uniforms!"

"Anytime, Maddie. I'll be giving out costumes on the first day of school." Liann watched as Maddie yanked up her flag, taking care to duck the pole through the door horizontally, but nearly knocking the picture frame off Liann's desk behind her.

&

Jake followed the road toward home, but instead of continuing past Rivers Honey, he turned his truck and took the driveway up to the Rivers' house. Practice had ended for the day, and he'd stopped by The Pit and purchased three barbecue orders to take home—two for supper tonight and one for lunch tomorrow. Nothing beat The Pit's smoked barbecue, corn on the cob, seasoned beans, and melt-in-your mouth ribs. The aroma made his mouth water, and he almost sneaked a rib from the box to munch on. He restrained himself as he put the truck in PARK.

Maddie had already asked if she could get a ride home from a friend after they went to get cherry limeades, so he figured this was the best time to talk to Liann about Maddie and color guard. Every night this week so far, his sister had come home sweating and cranky. He'd banished the flag from the wide veranda out back after Maddie nearly took out the lamp that hung from the veranda ceiling.

The Rivers' vehicles made a neat little row—Bert's pickup, Chin Mae's tiny gold car, and Liann's T-bird, at last freed from the shop. A new alternator had done the trick.

Jake gazed at the boxes of food on the front seat. This wouldn't take long, and he'd be home again, sitting at the supper table with Maddie.

He knocked on the back door, and Chin Mae answered. "You looking for Liann?"

"Yes, ma'am. I just need to talk with her for a few minutes."

"Liann!" Chin Mae flung the word over her shoulder. "You boyfriend's here!"

Jake opened his mouth a fraction then figured he'd let the label slide. He knew ladies like her quite well. Starlight was full of them. You started protesting about any matchmaking, and they started nosing deeper to see if there was a grain of truth in the protest. He liked Liann Rivers, quite a bit. During practice, he'd find his attention wandering to the marching band practicing in the parking lot on their marks. So far, the color guard hadn't joined the band in rehearsals. In time they would, with their vividly colored flags and graceful accents to the music.

"Jake, hi." Liann appeared in the doorway now, her face flushed. "Um, what brings you here?"

"I wanted to talk to you for a few minutes." He rubbed his chin then glanced across to the beehives studding the field. "I hope I'm not interrupting. Have you had supper yet?"

"No, we're eating later. Too hot, said my aunt. So I've sort of just nibbled." Her eyes were full of questions. "What's up?"

"Can we take a short walk?"

"No problem." Liann exited the house, scraping her hair back with an elastic scrunchie. "I can take you to see the bees if you like. I need to check the feeders on the boxes and let Uncle Bert know if we need to mix more feed." Her voice had a lilting tone, as if she were teasing him to see if he'd take her up on the offer.

"Okay. Lead the way." They crossed the front yard, full of Chin Mae's landscaping handiwork.

"You stay where I can see you!" Chin Mae's voice rang out. "No hanky-panky."

"She's safe with me, ma'am," Jake replied, laughing as Liann's face bloomed red.

"You'll have to excuse her." Liann stepped carefully over a rocky part of ground hidden under the grass. "She's. . .well. . . She's Aunt Chin Mae."

"She and Aunt Azalea are best friends for a reason." He squinted, regretting that he'd left his sunglasses in the truck. "They both lack subtlety with those big hearts of theirs."

"That's the truth." Liann stopped at the nearest stacked white boxes. A few bees lingered at the hive opening. She swallowed and hoped her nervousness didn't show. This was a stupid idea. She took a deep breath and touched Jake's arm. "Don't block their flight path. That's where we get the word 'beeline.'" She pointed to a lone bee traveling away from the hive. "It's like an invisible road they travel to collect the pollen. When you get in their way, it makes them nervous, my aunt says."

"Flight path, huh?" He looked down at her hand, still on his arm. "You sound like an expert."

Liann shook her head. "Nope, I'm not. I've had a crash course, though." She removed her hand from his arm and looked up at him. "So, you didn't come to talk about our crazy aunts or bees."

"No, I came to talk to you about Maddie." He waited for her response.

Liann moved closer to the hive and studied an inverted honey jar, partially full of what looked like a clear liquid. "I'll need to fill these tomorrow morning. We'll definitely need more feed."

"Maddie's a bright, intelligent girl, but I think she's a little impulsive sometimes." Jake walked beside Liann to the next hive. He sure wished she'd quit examining the hives. He wanted to see those dark eyes with laughter inside them.

"You're right. Maddie's very smart," Liann said as she straightened up from studying the next hive's feeder. "But when she talked to me about her decision to join color guard, she sounded like she'd thought it through very carefully."

"She talked to you about it? She must have told you about me wanting her to quit."

Liann nodded, the sunlight shining off her inky hair. "She was afraid I'd cut her from the squad."

"Can you?" Jake raised his eyebrows. Seemed like Maddie talked to everybody but him.

"Look, Jake. I've already been told that if I don't make this team work, it's axed next year. I only have eight girls, and all eight of them are counting on me. They work hard. They're all learning, including Maddie. I need all of them, every single one." She bit her lip and looked away from him.

What was it she was keeping from him? What was it that made this seem more than just a sport to her? Something else was at stake inside her. "But. . .what is it you're not telling me?"

"You're a coach, Jake. You specialize in winning. You want only the best, and you keep only the best. Or, you keep those that you think have potential. I get that." Liann continued to the next hive, and he followed, making sure he stayed out of the sacred flight path. "But some of these girls think they're the losers. They're not graceful enough to be on the dance squad, they're not athletic enough for the cheerleading squad. They love the music, though. Have you seen the band march and perform, with a full color guard? The guard helps make the music something more. I can't toss them out because they don't measure up to perfection."

Jake swallowed hard. "Why does this mean so much to you, personally? Because I feel like somehow, it does."

Liann ambled toward a wooden bench under the shade of an ancient live oak that was probably around during the time of the Alamo. She sat down, as did Jake. The land sloped away from them to the west, and the sun slid toward the horizon.

"You're right. It does mean something to me." Liann sighed. "I used to be in color guard my freshman year of high school. Someone made fun of me, made fun of our group, and I realized we probably looked like dorks. I was embarrassed. So after freshman year, I determined by that fall I'd make the cheerleading squad. I did. Varsity, as a sophomore. Unheard of in our school district. I left my old friends behind because I thought I'd gained something with my new status, something they didn't deserve. Nobody would lump me in with the dorks anymore." She fell silent.

He didn't know what to say, except to think that she was very driven, even back then. "You were young. Kids that age do a lot of things to impress the crowd. I see it all the time."

"But that doesn't make it right, then or now. I called myself a Christian, went to church regularly, participated in youth group and missions fund-raising. But I never looked at how I treated other people in my push to make the 'in' crowd."

Liann looked at him, her dark-brown eyes soft. "That's why I'm not cutting Maddie, or any girl. I can't ask her to leave, not to please you."

"I understand that." He'd seen a few guys come up the ranks: the scrappy guy who wanted to be a linebacker, the klutz who wanted to be a kicker. He'd also felt the pressure as a coach. A winning team meant scholarships for boys who might not otherwise have a chance to go to college. There certainly wasn't much in Starlight to keep kids here, not if they wanted to make a decent living, unless they were in the military, in business for themselves, were employed by the city or state, or worked for a military contractor.

He'd felt the pressure on both sides. Succeed and win, make a difference in their lives. But you couldn't do that with boys who didn't have the skills for football and were more legends in their own minds than real players on the field. If he had a winning team this year, it was his ticket to better things than Starlight.

"I'm sorry if that bothers you." She turned away. "You make your living by winning, not by keeping people who aren't cutting it."

"No, it doesn't bother me, not in this case," he admitted. "But back to Maddie. . . I wish she'd understand that every choice she makes has consequences. She shouldn't lose her focus on her goals. What if she starts slacking off?"

"Wow, you sound like her father, Jake." Liann chuckled, and the sound made him grit his teeth. Her smile tugged at him, too. "Let the girl breathe. She already told me she's in the top ten percent of her class. That's got to count for something."

"Well, it does. It means she shouldn't waste her potential."

He regretted the statement as soon as the words fell out of his mouth.

Liann stood. "Waste her potential? So you mean she's not just wasting her time but her potential in my class? Wow, and school hasn't even started yet." She hopped off the bench and started back toward the house, her legs moving at a brisk pace.

He caught up with her easily enough. "No, that's not what I meant."

She stopped by his truck and whirled to face him. "Then what did you mean?"

Jake felt the beginnings of a stammer on his lips, something that didn't happen often, and he closed his mouth.

"That's what I thought." Liann backed away, toward the house. "If you have any questions about Maddie's progress in my class, call me at the office after school starts. We'll be extremely busy in color guard, working hard. . .and wasting our time."

five

The kitchen door banged shut behind Liann, and she flinched. "Sorry!"

"You buying us a new door?" Aunt Chin Mae stood at the counter mixing up more kimchi. A pile of fresh vegetables, sliced and diced finely, made a rainbow of color on the cutting board.

"No." Liann took a deep breath and went to the fridge for a bottle of water.

"Trouble with your boyfriend?"

"He's not my boyfriend. He's. . . I've only known him a week, Aunt Chin Mae." Liann held back, not wanting to spew all the adjectives she wanted to tag him with. *Rude, pompous, condescending, control freak.*

"A week's long enough for me to see you two got something, maybe."

"I don't know about that. We sort of disagree right now about his sister." She unscrewed the cap on the water bottle and took a sip.

"Well, your uncle and I disagree about football teams. Always will. I can't stand those Dallas Cowboys." Her aunt shook her head.

"You'll come around, eventually," Uncle Bert called from the living room.

"Silly man!" Aunt Chin Mae shook a spatula in his direction. "It's been over thirty years. I'm not liking any Cowboys. I still like Patriots."

43

"They're not Texan." Uncle Bert huffed.

"I know. I like the name, Patriots. Men who love their country. Plus Tom Brady is cute."

"You two. . ." Liann laughed in spite of her thundercloud mood. She didn't want to say that disagreeing about a football team was entirely different from her disagreement with Jake. His words stung and smarted on her heart even now. In spite of his occasional flickers of borderline arrogance, she found him charming. However, she'd canceled a wedding two months ago. Even if she and Jake agreed about Maddie, she wasn't ready to jump into anything just yet. Also, he was probably only interested in her right now because she was his sister's teacher.

Her aunt scooped the vegetables into a mammoth plastic bowl and stirred the contents.

"Come taste the kimchi."

"I don't like kimchi." Liann tried not to make a face at the mixture of pickled vegetables in pungent brine. Her mother ate the stuff three times a day.

"You need to try it. What kind your mother make?"

"Cabbage." Now Liann did make a face.

"Ahh, I see." Aunt Chin Mae nodded. "You need to try different kimchi. This is cabbage, but I put radish and carrot in, too. It's sweeter. Here." She picked up a clean spoon.

"I'll try it once." Liann thought of something tastier, like chocolate pie, anything chocolate, and put the bite in her mouth. She tasted the heat and spice from the red pepper, the garlic and ginger. Then came a sweetness from the radish and carrot.

"So?"

"It's. . . It's good." She peeked at the bowl. "There's broccoli in it, too?"

"A little bit of everything." Aunt Chin Mae beamed. "See? You already discovering more about yourself. Coming to Texas is not a waste after all."

Liann laughed. "No, I guess not. My mother has been trying to get me to eat it for years."

"Now I get you some rice and another scoop of kimchi. You can take it to your room. Or I can heat up a frozen dinner." Aunt Chin Mae and Uncle Bert had a selection of frozen dinners to rival any grocer's freezer. "But kimchi's better for your digestive system. Keeps you cleansed."

"Thanks, Aunt Chin Mae, but no. I might get something later. I'm going to head to my room and relax." She needed to shower then check her e-mails.

"You need to find some friends here," said Aunt Chin Mae. "You need to get out of the house, do something. Every night it's the same. You come home, eat, then go to sleep."

"I'll find some friends. Don't worry about me. This is our busy season," Liann admitted. "Then next week it's nine-to-nine camp where we work the kids every day. We need to be ready for the opening game of the season in two weeks."

Uncle Bert entered the kitchen and stopped at the stove. "I got us season tickets, Mae."

"I don't know if I want to sit on metal bleachers for three hours every Friday night. What if it rains?"

"Honey, we can wear rain ponchos. They'll stop the game if there's lightning." Uncle Bert looked at Liann and winked. "Right, Li?"

"A little rain won't hurt anyone." She grinned back at him. "I'll holler at you all before I turn in for the night."

"You take care now." Uncle Bert waved.

Liann carried her bottle of water across to the two-story

garage. Her uncle had converted the second floor to a mini apartment that they rented out sometimes or opened for ministers who visited their church. Already, she felt like she could breathe a little easier.

She pounded up the stairs and felt her phone buzz in her pocket. She glanced at the number before entering the apartment. Jake. She ignored the call. She wasn't ready to talk to him, yet, although she knew eventually she would have to. A blast of cool air hit her as she opened the door. She'd turned the thermostat on the AC to eighty degrees, which still felt cool compared to outside.

Liann sank onto the love seat, leaned toward the coffee table, and turned on her laptop computer. Six months ago, she never imagined she'd be here. Texas. No wedding. A part-time job doing color guard that had her working sixty hours a week. And a new job helping with the bees. Again, the questions—no, prayer—ringing in her mind. *Lord, what's going on? Did I make this decision in haste?*

Her phone buzzed again. Matt. She'd been avoiding him long enough after the confrontation that sent her packing, literally. She pushed the button. "Hi, Matt."

"Liann. Hi. You're finally answering the phone."

"I've been busy with my new job."

"I wanted to make sure you were okay."

"I'm doing great." *Lord, I hope that doesn't count as a lie.* She had a roof over her head, family who loved her. A career that had hit a bump in the road, but she was making the best of it. A lot of people had it worse. Yes, she was doing great when she stopped to count her blessings.

"Good. I'm glad. It's good to hear your voice."

Matt didn't do small talk, so Liann braced herself for

whatever came next. "Thanks."

"I've been praying, Liann, and I really believe that God wants us back together. I know every couple has doubts sometimes. They work through them. I know I have no doubt in my mind that I want to work through things with you, to have you by my side in whatever the Lord has in store for us." He fell silent, and for a few seconds Liann wondered if they'd lost their connection.

She looked at her phone. Nope, the call timer still ticked along. How long had he practiced those words? He definitely sounded genuine. Not that she doubted his love for her at all.

"I'm sure you have prayed about it, and I believe that you're sincere." Liann swallowed her sigh. "What's my favorite food, Matt?"

"What does that have to do with anything? We're so good together. With your determination and energy, you'll make an ideal youth pastor's wife. You're great with young people and will be an ideal mentor to them. Don't let fear keep you from responding to your calling."

"How do I like my eggs cooked, Matt?" She snatched a line from the movie *Runaway Bride*. "Scrambled, sunny-side up, over easy. . .or do I hate eggs?"

"Me knowing how you like your eggs cooked has nothing to do with having a good marriage." She didn't miss the sharpness that crept into his voice.

"Yes, it does." She'd never had a conversation like this with him before.

"Liann, I love you. So much. I don't know or understand what you're going through. But I'll wait. I'll wait for you."

"You don't have to wait. I do care for you, but I don't love you enough to marry you."

"Give it time. I pray that God will show you the way." With that, he hung up. He'd had the last word, of course.

Matt—dynamic, charismatic, with eyes for her alone. She should have guessed that he didn't want her opinion. He assumed he knew what she wanted. And she? Well, she'd gone along with the romance of it all. Cheerleading coach falls in love with up-and-coming youth pastor, and they transform the next generation with their mentoring and discipleship and go on to raise two-point-five children. And a dog. She wanted a dog, but Matt didn't want pets. That should have been a clue. It was always what Matt wanted, never what she preferred.

Nope, she wouldn't let a man do her thinking for her or let him skew her thinking again. With Jake, she had to admit it was a little different. Right from the "git-go," as Uncle Bert would say, she'd been forthright with her opinions about Maddie and color guard, just as he'd been very clear about his. He didn't seem like a malicious man who was adept at flinging veiled barbs that carried his real feelings.

Not that anything was brewing with Jake Tucker, of course, no matter what her aunt believed.

❧

"So I told Liann I didn't want Maddie to waste her potential," Jake told his brother, Billy.

"Bro, you sure stuck your foot in it this time." Billy glanced at his wife, Justine, as they stood just inside his office doorway. Funny, they never came by the athletic office.

"Jake, did you realize how that might have sounded to Liann?" Justine shook her head, her blond waves cascading over her shoulders. She leaned on Billy then looked up at him. "I would have called Billy out if he'd said something like that."

"Well, I figured it out, as soon as I said it." He still felt the heat from Liann's crackling gaze, followed by a glimpse of hurt just as she turned away. "I tried to say something, but. . . Well, she walked off."

Really, everyone was making it sound like they'd had some type of couple's spat. Which it wasn't. He glared at the playbook on his desk.

Lunch break was short. They waited until one o'clock to take a break, when the heat of the day was approaching its worst. This afternoon after lunch, they'd review video of old plays and maybe watch some playoff games to motivate the kids. Then would come weight lifting in the gym and a few drills at twilight.

"So, have you called her to apologize, or at least explain?" Justine stood up straight, crossing her arms across her chest.

"I tried. Once. She didn't answer." Jake glanced at the large digital clock on the wall, ticking away the minutes of the lunch break. "And I've been busy lately. So has she."

"That parking lot's not so big that you can't walk across it," said Billy.

"Like I said, I've been busy." Ten minutes, and he'd round up the guys with the rest of the coaching staff. "So, why else are you here today? I don't think you came to inhale the aroma of sweaty athletes."

"No, are you kidding? The hallway smells like Fritos, but I wasn't going to say anything. Except maybe leave a container of Febreze on your desk." Justine grinned at him then turned to Billy.

"Well, uh," Billy said, rubbing his hand on his unruly hair. His little brother wore the same look the year that he'd unwrapped all the Christmas presents then hid them again.

Jake could've throttled him then. Now, though. . .

"Is everything okay? Y'all aren't moving away, are you? I mean, couldn't blame you. LA seems a lot more exciting than Starlight."

"We're pregnant!" Justine squealed then clamped her hands over her mouth. "I just found out. Little Peanut is super young—six weeks, if that."

Jake pushed back from his desk and met Billy and Justine on the other side. He grabbed Billy and wrapped him in a hug. "Bubbas. . . Wow, my Bubbas is going to be a daddy. Wow." His eyes burned, and he blinked. "C'mere you," he said as he reached for Justine, giving her a quick hug and a peck on the cheek. "Congratulations, y'all. Wow. I'm gonna be an uncle." He paced in front of his desk.

"We're going to tell Mom and Dad tonight, on Skype." Billy tugged Justine close to his side. "We weren't planning on starting a family so soon, with Justine's shooting schedule for the show this fall, but—"

"The producer will work around it." Justine shrugged, her grin widening. "I was shocked, too. But I can't wait!" She placed her hand on her stomach.

"When are you telling Maddie?" Jake knew Maddie would hate to be out of the loop.

"We were going to tell her before we tell Mom and Dad, but I think we'll tell her now, too. Is she over at the gymnasium?" asked Billy.

"She should be. They're practicing until late tonight."

"Good. We'll head there right now." Billy gave Justine an adoring look, and she popped up on her tiptoes and kissed him.

"See y'all later." Jake watched them leave the office.

He didn't fully understand how the one-time megastar

Justine Campbell had adapted to life in Texas for over a year now, but her marriage to his brother had a lot to do with it. She would jet off sometimes to film her reality-based human interest show, *Second Chances*. After the first season, the going buzz was that an Emmy nomination waited in her future.

Billy couldn't have done better for himself, and Justine adored the what-you-see-is-what-you-get with Billy. His brother had been through a lot, laying his life on the line for his country during three tours in Iraq. He earned a Purple Heart that he never talked about but kept tucked in a drawer somewhere. Jake glanced up at the shelf of coaching awards and plaques. How did awards that would tarnish compare to finding true love? Maybe Billy did right, keeping his medals in a drawer.

Billy was right, too, that Jake had misstepped with Liann. One thing was for sure: he'd apologize. Not to get everyone off his back, but because he hadn't meant to hurt her feelings. Sometimes, things just came out wrong. He could bark out football plays and give motivational spiels to the team, but in other matters he was just as prone to foot-in-mouth syndrome as other men.

At twilight, while the guys were running the field, Jake excused himself and left them under the watchful eye of another assistant coach. He crossed the steaming parking lot. If someone felt like fried eggs for supper, all they needed was the eggs, a frying pan, and a patch of asphalt.

Jake entered the gymnasium and immediately heard the strains of "Beauty and the Beast." He pictured the hairy beast in a fancy outfit, whirling around the ballroom with Belle. Maddie had watched the DVD thousands of times and sang the songs around the house when she was little.

He'd had his fill of it one summer break during his college years. Now that the band was playing the music, she'd started listening to it all over again.

Liann had her back to him, her hands on her hips, a flag on the floor by her feet. "That's it. . . . Line up even. . . . Spin, spin, spin. . . . Wait for the crescendo, and you'll hear the trumpets. . .and throw—*yes!*" The girls, in unison, tossed their flags, which spiraled above their heads, then dropped into their waiting hands. "Beautiful!"

One flag crashed on the floor. Maddie's. She glared at the flag then glanced in his direction, and she froze like a mama deer in the field.

Liann looked over her shoulder, her own eyes widening. She reached for a CD player on a wheeled cart and pushed a button. The music stopped. "Ladies, take a quick break. Five minutes."

Maddie glared again at her flag before she walked off with a tall brunette. A stream of giggles followed the girls to the water fountain in the hallways.

"Hi, Jake." Liann wiped her forehead with the back of her hand. "Everything okay?"

"Yes. No." He glanced toward the hallway. A pair of heads peeked around the corner then darted away. "Listen. I'm sorry about what I said the other day. I wasn't thinking."

"Apology accepted. I, um, probably overreacted a little bit." She placed a hand on the CD player. "You *did* call. Then I got busy, and, well. . .you know."

"I do know." He took a step closer. "Y'all were doing a good job. It's amazing what you've been able to do with them in such a short time."

She smiled at him, and her expression reminded him of

Justine's when she looked at Billy. Uh-oh. His heart skipped a beat.

"It's a work in progress. I started with the middle part. . . the love song. We're going to backtrack with the opening section—'Belle.' It's peppier, and there's more complicated runs. A couple of the juniors are spinning rifles on that one, which is a review for me, too."

"Uh, about Maddie. Looks like she's still having a hard time."

"I'm not cutting her." Liann's response peppered the air.

"No, I'm not asking you to." Jake cleared his throat. "But I'd like you to come to our house this weekend, if you want to. Maybe if you and Maddie work together, it'll help her."

Liann blinked at him. "Are you sure your name is Jake Tucker? Because not five days ago you were trying to talk me into getting her off the team."

"I'm going to give her a chance. Maddie's a perfectionist and doesn't have a high tolerance for frustration. If she thinks she's not going to succeed, she'll back down. And I won't have to talk anyone out of anything." He couldn't believe he'd just invited Liann to the house. Maybe Billy and Justine could come—run interference or something. Then someone would have to clean. With his and Maddie's schedules lately, no one had vacuumed or loaded the dishwasher. The trash can brimmed with take-out boxes. Mom would, as Maddie put it, "have a cow" at the state of her once-beloved home.

"You sly dog." Liann shook her head. "You tell me what date and time, and I'll be there. Maddie's going to make a breakthrough. You'll see. I just know it."

She reached out and gave him a playful shove. Before Jake

could stop himself, he reached out and grabbed her hand. He squeezed it. A few giggles echoed through the gym.

Glen, one of his assistants, stuck his head into the gym. "Tucker, we've got Kansas Tech Athletics on the line for you."

"Guess you'd better take that call." Liann pulled her hand back. But she smiled at him. "It sounds important, if Kansas is calling."

"I hope so." He felt himself grinning like a boy on the first day of summer vacation. "I'll call and let you know."

six

Trixie refused to start on Saturday afternoon. That figured, with Biff's Auto Shop closed for the weekend. Which meant unless Liann called Jake for a ride, she'd either hoof it, which didn't appeal to her at all, or take Aunt Chin Mae's Smart Car. Uncle Bert was playing dominoes at the Bushes' place.

"You use my car anytime you need, Liann," her aunt had said.

She never imagined anytime to be now, with the mercury still hovering around one hundred degrees. Did this place *ever* cool off? She never remembered Texas being quite this hot when visiting as a kid. Liann picked up a practice flag then glanced at the wooden rifle in the corner. Maybe she'd bring it, and the saber, too. Just in case.

"Take good care of my car," Aunt Chin Mae said when Liann went to gather the keys from the hook on the kitchen wall. "Bring it back in one piece."

"I will. I'm just going down the road a little ways." Liann picked up her aunt's key chain with the green plastic frog on the end. "I won't be too late."

"Don't worry about it. You a grown woman. I won't call and check up on you like your mother would." Aunt Chin Mae waved her off. "Have fun visiting your boyfriend and his family."

"He's not my boyfriend." Liann shook her head and laughed. She left the house and ambled to the driveway.

Aunt Chin Mae's tiny gold vehicle glinted in the sunlight. It looked sort of like a metallic bean on wheels.

She scooted into the Smart Car and laid the rifle and saber in the passenger seat. However, the flag was way too long for a two-seater. Liann rolled up the flag and stuck it through the open window on the passenger side. So long as it didn't unravel and start flapping in the breeze like the sail of a ship, she'd be in good shape heading over to the Tuckers' house.

The inside was like a sports car—comfortable, with bucket seats. Liann eased down the driveway, feeling as if she piloted a pod craft in space. She headed along the road toward Tucker Ranch, taking care not to hit the occasional hole in the asphalt.

Liann eased the car over the cattle guard, the wheels bouncing on the metal pipes covering the driveway. The car gave a little pop as the rear wheels rolled back onto solid pavement.

She was right on time. A shiny blue pickup truck sat beside a small limestone building with another sign: TUCKER BOOTS. She didn't recall seeing it the other day in her dehydrated fog. What didn't this family do? No wonder Maddie was so driven. Tuckers didn't sit around for long—or if they did, they were probably planning something.

Liann parked the Smart Car next to what she guessed was Jake's truck. Maddie bounded out the front door of the long ranch house and was at the driver's side door before Liann could turn off the engine.

"You made it," Maddie said as soon as Liann climbed out of the car. "Wow, now that's what I call a metallic paint job."

"Yes, my aunt's car. Mine wouldn't start again, but I didn't want to miss coming tonight." Liann had to smile at her enthusiasm. "Tonight is when everything changes for you. You're going to do great."

"I hope so."

Maddie led her not to the house but to a wooden barn that dwarfed the small limestone building beside it. "Jake's in here. He asked if I'd take you over here when you arrived." They entered the barn, and Liann squinted to see with the help of the sunlight slanting over their shoulders. Six stalls plus a hayloft made up the interior.

"Hey, do you like horseback riding?" Jake pushed a wheelbarrow into the center of the wide aisle.

"I've ridden a few times, mostly the old, slow horses on trail rides. Nothing too adventurous, but I enjoy it." Liann thought they'd be visiting inside or practicing with the flags outside.

"She can ride Misty. I don't mind." Maddie tugged on Liann's arm. "She's really gentle and sweet. I've had her since I was ten. She'll go wherever you want to go."

"Am I too early?" Liann asked.

"Not at all. We're sort of delayed. Billy and Justine are coming, too, but they're waiting to pick up a fresh pie from Rebecca's Kitchen in Kempner," Jake said, as if that explained everything. "Plus, *somebody* forgot to make their potato salad until the last minute." With this, he glanced at Maddie and gave her a grin that took any of the irritation out of his words.

"Okay." Horseback riding. She was wearing the black stretchy pants she used for working out and her sturdy sneakers. "But I don't have boots on."

Jake put a hand on his hip and swaggered in her direction. "Ma'am, that don't mean you can't go ridin' for a while."

"I'll get Misty saddled for you," Maddie said as she buzzed

off. "Then I'll go check on the potatoes."

Within fifteen minutes, Misty, the white placid mare, and Patch, Jake's horse, were saddled and ready to mount. Liann managed to haul herself up onto Misty's back. The mare looked shorter than she really was. Liann gripped the saddle horn with one hand and clenched the reins with the other.

"Don't worry. When she sees Patch step out, she'll go, too. She'll follow him wherever he goes." Jake looked as comfortable as a real cowboy on his horse's back. Patch was taller still than Misty, white with brown splotches on his body, legs, face, and neck. He gave a little kick, and Jake settled back in the saddle.

"I hope Misty doesn't follow his lead, not that way."

"Oh, she won't." Jake reined Patch back until Misty ambled her way in his direction. Liann scanned the land, dotted with live oaks, twelve to fifteen feet tall, along with green scraggly cedar bushes of varying heights. Those bushes, she'd learned from Uncle Bert, were the source of many central Texans' allergies and the reason that Rivers Honey did so well. The land looked unspoiled, covered with dry grass and studded with rocks. Liann guessed it probably looked the same a hundred years ago. She remembered Uncle Bert telling her all about the real cowboys of Texas.

"How many acres do you have?" Liann tried to let Misty's soft swaying motion relax her back.

"Sixty-five. Our land ends at the Lampasas River." Jake released some of the tension on Patch's reins, and the horse tossed his head.

"What are those three little cottages over there? My aunt mentioned that your brother runs a soldiers' ranch here."

"New Hope Ranch—that's Billy's project. He and Justine

run a nonprofit that invites recovering soldiers and their families to spend weekends here on the ranch." Jake brought Patch to a halt, and Misty stopped as well. "The second building was recently finished this spring. We had a wet spring, so building stopped for a while. Otherwise we would've been done sooner."

"The cottages are really cute." Liann wanted to hop off Misty and look in the porch window of the first cottage, but then she'd be faced with having Jake help her get back on. As it was, riding like this with him felt almost. . .like a date. Maybe it was just to kill time, but they could have done that in the air-conditioned house. They reached a stand of tall oak trees that arched over the trail and gave them some dappled shade.

"We'll be at the river soon," Jake said as the horses strolled along under the high branches. "I remember getting some good catfish out of there back when I was in high school."

"Do you still fish there?" One thing Liann liked was fishing. Not that she'd had the chance very often, but she and her parents would go sometimes to the mountains. Mom would try to teach her how to cook, and Dad would teach her how to fish. The camping she wasn't so crazy about, but she loved the feel of reeling in a fish, wrestling to get it into the net.

"It's been awhile."

"Why'd you stop?" She glanced at him. He looked deep in thought, his hazel eyes focused on the saddle horn.

"I don't know. Got busy, I guess." He shrugged and looked her way.

"I love fishing. I find it relaxing." She found herself smiling at the admission. "Like you, I got busy, though."

"You, fish? I wouldn't have picked you for a fisherperson." For the first time, Liann realized he had a dimple in one cheek. Maybe because today she was seeing relaxed Jake, away from the field and the pressure he loved so much.

"Why not?"

"I dunno. It doesn't seem like. . .you. I can see you being a cheerleader and doing the whole spirit thing, and backflips and pyramids. But fishing?"

"Yup." The wide path grew rockier as they headed downhill. The broad trail gave them plenty of room to ride, but it was an ideal route for runoff from the rain. Which, of course, ran straight to the river.

"Almost there." Jake didn't look back but kept his attention on the trail ahead. "Careful. It's a little trickier going down."

"I'll just let Misty do her thing." Liann had hardly needed to lean the reins on Misty's neck. "She's done great so far without my help." The shadows had grown longer as they'd ridden the distance from the house.

"Here we are." Patch came to a halt, and Jake swung off his back. "You going to get off for a few minutes, stretch your legs?"

"Um, sure." Liann pulled back on Misty's reins, but Misty had already clumped to a halt. She slid down from Misty's back, and the horse put her head down and started sniffing for scraps of grass. The sound of gurgling water filled the air as sunlight glinted off the river.

"What about the horses?"

"Patch won't leave, and wherever he is, Misty will be." Jake looped Patch's reins over a low branch. "I forgot how much I like these cliffs. I used to come down here and find fossils in the limestone, besides catch fish." He stepped from the sheltering shade of the oaks and onto a large flat rock that jutted out into the river. Jake pointed up to the cliffs.

Liann joined him on the rock and followed his line of sight. The river, over hundreds of years, had carved a slow but definite space in the limestone, and the cliff on the opposite side of the river rose at least twenty feet above their heads. The river itself was barely more than a foot deep, probably no more than three feet in the center. The current drifted lazily, inviting her to toss an inner tube onto the surface of the water and drift along.

"What kind of fossils?" She almost wanted to find a place to cross the river and start chipping at the limestone herself. Their side of the riverbank sloped gently to meet the water, which was dotted with small rocks.

"Clams, mostly, of all sizes. A few trilobites." He grinned. "My dad left some of the fossils on the mantel in the living room. This poor river is so dry. You can tell it's the middle of August, and we haven't had any rain for at least a month. When the drought was really bad, the river was almost a trickle." Jake used his hand to shield his eyes as he looked downstream.

"I can't wait until it cools off more around here."

"Not till mid-September, at least. Those first few games are going to be scorchers."

"Speaking of football, you got a phone call from Kansas Tech the other day. You seemed pretty excited about it."

"Yes. They're sending a coaching scout to watch one of the Yellowjackets games sometime in the next few weeks. They're recruiting for their coaching staff, and I found out they're considering me. My head coach knows, so the process is going smoothly so far." He grinned and picked up a small rock, chucking it into the river. "Then, if Starlight makes the Division 4A playoffs, I could be offered a spot higher up. Away from here, finally."

"But you love it here." Liann tried not to frown. "I can hear it when you talk about coming to this place to fish, when you talk to my aunt and uncle, or the Bushes."

"I've always wanted to coach at the NCAA level. It's been a dream since I was a kid. Usually coaches from larger school districts get considered, but my college buddy is on the staff there, and he put in a good word for me. I'm counting on a great season this fall. The boys have it. I can tell."

"I see." Why did her heart sink just a little at the idea of him leaving Starlight? After all, two weeks ago she'd been considering this a temporary exile. That is, until she realized she wanted to prove to the town that the color guard squad would work—that these girls weren't losers.

Until she met Jake.

"Yup." Jake snapped his fingers then slapped his fist with his palm of the opposite hand. "Have you ever wanted something, prayed for it, worked for it? You can see it right there, in front of you, just out of reach? But you know in your heart, it's yours. . .someday?"

"I—I'm not sure." The truth hurt her ears. What had she truly ever wanted? Had she ever tried to dream big like Jake? Cheerleading had started out as a social climbing move on her part. She'd done it for selfish and shallow reasons. Then she'd drifted into college with the promise of eventually teaching and coaching secondary school, which she loved. Then the new youth pastor came on board at her church. After a whirlwind romance, a proposal, then—here. Almost twenty-seven years old.

"I do. I can see it happening, someday soon. Maybe that's why I was hard on Maddie. Because I hit the big 3-0, my last birthday. It sort of sneaks up on you, you know? I don't want her to start making compromises and settling, because life happens fast. Look at what happened to Billy. Less than three years ago, he was trying to get his life back after a roadside bomb in Iraq almost killed him. Now he's married, going to be a father. He's running a terrific nonprofit that really helps people." Jake turned to step off their perch on the rock, and Liann moved to let him pass. His boot slipped, and he reached to catch himself with a free hand. Patch's head jerked up, and Jake skittered back at Patch's sudden movement, watching the reins sliding quick as a noodle from the tree branch. On his powerful haunches, Patch tore up the trail toward the house with Misty right behind him.

"Patch! Misty!" Jake regained his balance before completely falling. Liann reached for his arm as if she could keep his two hundred pounds from landing half on the bank of the river and half on the rock. Then she slipped, and they both tumbled into the shallow water.

"Ow!" Liann felt a chuckle erupt, and she flung water on Jake as she lay half on her side on some rocks, half on his arm.

"What was that for?" he asked.

"Taking me riding before supper. It's hot outside, and I knew this was a bad idea." She flung more water on him as she sat upright. The cool water chased away the prickly heat feeling, but another heat crept into her cheeks. Then a wave of river water struck her in the face, and she couldn't breathe.

"There, feel better?" Jake started laughing himself.

Coughing and spluttering, Liann swept her arm under

the water and responded with a wave of her own that struck Jake's head and shoulders. She laughed at the look on his face, and the laughter felt good. She couldn't remember the last time she'd laughed so hard. "You're acting like a big kid."

"I am when I'm here." The sunlight sparkled off his hazel eyes as he pulled her close to him and kissed her.

Kissing Jake was like Fourth of July fireworks, riding a roller coaster, and standing at the edge of a roaring ocean all at once. Liann heard the river gurgling, felt the wet denim of Jake's shirt collar. With one of his arms around her, she felt like nothing else mattered at the moment—not her crazy job situation, her broken engagement, her—

Liann pulled back, breathless. "Not fair, Jake Tucker. So not fair." She sat up straight, her knees bent.

※

Jake would've kissed her again if she hadn't pulled away from him, looking like a scolding teacher. He touched her cheek. "I've wanted to do that since. . .since the morning we met each other, running."

"You're not playing fair, Jake." Liann stood up, water streaming from her pants and weighing down her shirt. "You talk about leaving Starlight, and now *this*."

"It's just a simple kiss," he said, trying to get his footing and onto dry land. "It sort of, uh, seemed like a good idea at the moment."

"Well, most people don't go around kissing people like—like *that*—just because 'it seemed like a good idea at the moment.'" She tugged on her sleeves that clung to her arms then squeezed the excess water from her hair. "Plus, there was nothing simple about it. We're not even. . . I don't know."

"Your aunt seems to think we're boyfriend and girlfriend."

He tried to reach for her hand, but she sidestepped away from him as neatly as Patch could.

"We're not." She started stomping down the path, leaving a stream of water behind her. "You can't just. . .kiss me like that."

"Liann Rivers, I like you. I like you a lot." The admission made him realize how foolish he'd been to reach for her and kiss her as if he had a right to do so. "I don't know what the future holds right now, but I like having you around. Maddie thinks the world of you. Every night it's 'Ms. Rivers this' and 'Ms. Rivers said that.'"

She paused on the path and faced him. "Jake. . . I like you, too. A lot. So far. But I'm probably not the best one to be going into a. . .relationship with right now."

"I know—you just moved here, you have a new job." He slipped his arm around her, and this time she didn't pull away. They continued along the trail back toward the house.

Then she stopped again and faced him. "That's true. But that's not all. I. . . I was supposed to have gotten married two months ago, in June. I—I called it off in May."

Liann, engaged? "Why did you call it off?"

"He was practically perfect. Driven, confident, passionate, loves young people. Just like you. In some ways, you remind me of him."

Jake could hear the death knell of what might have been. If she left that guy, practically at the altar, would she do the same to him? "I hear a 'but' coming."

"He always thought he knew best. For me. For both of us. Anytime I tried to voice my opinion, it was drowned out. At the time, I didn't realize it. Finally, an old friend of mine looked at our wedding website—"

"You had a *wedding website*?"

"Yes, we did." Liann sighed before continuing. "She told me she saw plenty of pictures of me, but there was nothing in that wedding that was *me*. Not the music. Or the cake or the dresses. I ran everything by Matt—"

"His name's Matt?" Jake felt a tendril of jealousy trying to wind itself around his heart and squeeze. A man he didn't even know, claiming Liann.

Liann nodded. "*Anyway*, I took a step back and realized she was pointing out the truth. Then I took another step back and realized I was aligning myself with Matt's dream. But it wasn't mine. He's a youth pastor. I love working with young people, but I would rather work with kids who wouldn't necessarily darken a church doorway. When I realized that. . . Oh, you should have heard the debates we had about *that*. Not long after that, I called off the wedding and started looking for jobs anywhere but California."

She paused at the sound of an engine, and Jake looked in its direction. Billy, coming along in his truck. He pulled up, a cloud of dust swirling around them.

"Y'all look like you're in a bind. Maddie caught the horses, so I figured I'd hop in the truck and see what became of you two." Billy gave Jake a pointed look, as if he knew *exactly* what had become of the two of them.

The wet denim of Jake's jeans and shirt pulled on his arms and legs as he drew closer to the truck. "Had a little mishap by the rocks. Slipped in, spooked Patch." He leaned on the hood and eyeballed the pristine leather interior.

"You can ride in the back, if you don't mind." Billy gestured with his head. "Wet denim and leather seats don't go together very well."

Jake glanced at Liann, who walked with him to the rear of the truck. He popped the gate down then helped her into the truck's bed. He climbed up behind her as she slid over to one side. She hugged her knees up to her chin. Water still dripped from their clothing.

Nope, this definitely wasn't the way he'd envisioned the evening unfolding for them. He wasn't sure exactly what he'd expected. He knew it would involve hearing the *Beauty and the Beast* music over and over, plus the flipping of flags and hopefully no broken glass anywhere. But not a kiss at the river.

Now Liann sat across from him, jostling with the movement of the truck, closed up tight as a clam. Her hair had already started to dry from the heat, and she ran her fingers through the dark strands. For the first time, Jake noted a reddish sheen to her hair, a trio of freckles on one cheek.

This was why he didn't let himself get distracted. She was right. It wasn't fair of him to kiss her. *Lord, help me make amends for this mistake.*

seven

Liann made it through supper, somehow, although the memory of Jake's kiss wouldn't leave her alone. Not that she or Jake had anything to feel guilty about. But she wasn't about to follow a man somewhere she wasn't ready to go herself. She folded her arms and leaned against the porch railing. Jake had made it clear he was on his way out of Starlight. And her? She was just here long enough to figure out what would come next for her. What the Lord had for her. So far, she wasn't sure she'd chosen wisely in coming to Texas.

"...isn't that right, Ms. Rivers?" Maddie asked.

"I'm sorry, could you repeat that question?" Liann looked across the porch at Maddie.

"I said that you brought your own equipment tonight so we can work on the routine together."

"Yes, I did." Liann stood. "Matter of fact, I can get them out of the car now so we can get started. After all, that's why I'm here." She dared not look at Jake. Fortunately, her clothing dried quickly, and she'd worn an old tracksuit of Mrs. Tucker's in the meantime. She'd felt like a sopping-wet waif next to the statuesque Justine Tucker, who still worked professionally as Justine Campbell. Of all the ways to make a good first impression on someone, returning waterlogged from a trail ride hadn't been one of them.

Liann trotted over to where Aunt Chin Mae's golden bean

was parked. Footsteps followed her. She didn't need to turn around to know they were Jake's.

"Are you okay?" He put one hand on the car's roof.

"I'm okay." She tugged the flag from the car window then reached inside to pull out the saber and rifle. "Really, I am."

"I wanted to make sure."

"It's probably best we pretend the whole thing never happened." She hugged the equipment to her chest. "We've got a busy fall ahead of us, and truthfully, neither of us knows what lies ahead. I prayed about coming here and thought every door opened. But it seems nothing's turned out like I thought it would."

Jake dug his toe in the dirt, turning over a rock. "I know. Life has a way of doing that. I thought I would have moved away from here sooner. Then Billy was injured in Iraq—nearly died. I stayed around to help when he came home. Then my dad got sick. Then Mom and Dad moved to Colorado because of his heart. I thought it would be easy to keep an eye on Maddie. She's a good kid. But I feel like I've been on hold here, waiting on everyone else. Doing the right thing."

"I know God will honor you for that. The right opportunity will come up for you, I'm sure. Like Kansas Tech." Now she understood his sense of urgency. "I imagine it seems like everyone else is moving on with their lives except you."

He shrugged. "Maybe. I know God does things in His time. Not sure what that means sometimes. Just when I think I'll have my chance, I hit another roadblock."

"I'm sorry. It must be hard." She started walking back toward the porch, minding the uneven ground.

"I pray and push through." He gave her half a grin as they reached the others.

Maddie stood in the yard, facing the porch. "Okay, y'all. I can't wait to show you what I've been learning. I have a lot to work on, but it's been fun."

"I'm glad you think so," Liann said as she stepped up next to Maddie. She laid the rifle and saber a safe distance away on the ground. "Let's start from the beginning. We'll go straight through from 'Belle' to 'Beauty and the Beast,' and then if you're game, I'll show you 'The Battle Scene.' We haven't gone over that in class yet, because it features the rifles and sabers."

Maddie started the music, and she and Liann started the first movements while Billy, Justine, and Jake watched from the porch. Liann kept an eye on Maddie, who only dropped the flag once during the peppy number.

"Good job!" Liann said, and Maddie glowed. The music transitioned to the slower song, a good chance for them to catch their breath and do some of the pretty flag work. At the crescendo, Maddie sent the flag arcing high above her, as did Liann.

Then Maddie missed the flag and it hit the ground, pole end first. The flag flipped end over end and lay in the grass. Maddie glared at it, and Liann punched the OFF button on the CD player.

"I'll never get this." Maddie stamped her foot on the grass.

"Don't worry about it, sweetie," Justine called out from the porch. "Liann is here to help you. Besides, what I saw was really pretty."

"That's right," Liann said. "Tell you what. Let's turn the music off and do some drills. You all might find this a little boring, since there's no choreography and no music. Just giving you a warning." She smiled at the audience on the porch.

Maddie stomped over to get her flag. "Okay, I'll try."

"That's the spirit," said Jake. He nodded at Liann. She was glad he knew the importance of pushing kids when they didn't think they were good. So often people gave up before their big breakthrough.

The realization hit her, even now. No, she wouldn't give up on Starlight. She'd see the fall season through, for the girls. Especially Maddie. Then, she'd see what came her way in the spring, after the football and marching competitions were over. That left preparation for the spring show and individual routines before the end of the school year.

They did their spin drills, but Maddie frowned when Liann said, "Okay, now we'll do some throws."

Maddie spun the flag, released it, then took half a step back before trying to catch it.

"Don't step back." Liann stopped spinning. "Now I see what you're doing. You're taking half a step back after you release the flag. It's not going to hit you."

"I know. But I can't help it." Maddie tried again, this time catching it successfully.

"Hang on a second." Liann noticed that the guys had gone inside the house, leaving Justine watching them. "Let's try a rifle."

"I don't know if I can. It looks more complicated to spin and throw that." Maddie bit her lip as Liann carried the wooden rifle back to their patch of practice lawn.

"Okay, watch." Liann started spinning the rifle, one direction only. It had taken her an hour last Saturday evening to get her old skills to kick in, but like the old riding-a-bicycle saying, her hands and reflexes remembered. She bounced it off one hand then reversed the spin direction. Then a flip, as the rifle spun in succession. Her hands stopped the movement, the wood hitting her palms with a snap.

"Wow." Maddie's eyes glowed.

Liann extended the rifle to Maddie. "Your turn. Think of it as a flag, only thicker, heavier, and shorter."

Maddie spun the rifle, and a slow smile spread across her face as she concentrated. Then she mimicked Liann, bouncing it off one hand and reversing direction. The tip of her tongue poked out from the corner of her mouth. Liann would definitely have to work on *that* with Maddie.

"Great job!" Liann glanced over at Justine, who applauded.

"This is so cool!" Maddie reversed the rifle's direction again, the spin turning into a white blur.

The front door opened, and the guys came out. One of them turned on the porch light. "Hey, we started cutting the pie," said Billy. "We couldn't take waiting anymore."

The men stopped and stared as Maddie flipped the rifle up in the air a few feet, using one hand. She reached out and it snapped back onto her hands. She whirled to face Liann. "I did it! I did it! Am I a natural?" She flung herself at Liann in a hug, dropping the rifle in the process.

Liann hugged Maddie and tried not to shoot Jake a look of triumph. "I guess you are." She had a feeling Maddie wouldn't be in a hurry to quit anytime soon.

Maddie did a little jig in the front yard, now nearly dark as twilight settled in the west. "I don't know what it was. It felt easier to spin the rifle. Maybe because it's shorter, more compact?"

"Well, you'll definitely have a role in the battle scene. I think I'll have three of you spin rifles, while five of you use the flags, or maybe sabers. It's the final movement, so we want it to be visually dramatic." Liann grinned at Maddie.

A pair of headlights shone down the driveway, and a four-door sedan rolled up to the other line of vehicles. Liann glimpsed the head and shoulders of a man. A young man.

"Hey, y'all," he said as he left the car. He looked comfortable in his Yellowjackets shirt and worn-out jeans.

"Tim Rollins." Maddie clamped her hand on Liann's wrist. "Tim. At our house. And I feel and look like a sweat ball."

"What brings you by tonight?" asked Jake, strolling up to meet Tim at the edge of the drive.

"Hey, Coach." Tim dipped his head, making himself look shorter than Jake, even though they were of equal height. "I, uh. . . I wanted to say hi to Maddie. And you, too."

"Well, come on over, we're about ready to have some dessert." He clapped the young man on the shoulders.

"He came to see me." Maddie gave Liann a triumphant look and raced for the front door. "Be right back, y'all."

Liann felt unsettled in the pit of her stomach. Jake Tucker thought he could handle Maddie just fine while she finished school. Maybe last year had been smooth for the Tuckers. But Liann had the feeling that he hadn't ever tried to corral a teenage girl when boys entered the mix. School started Monday, and with it, a whole new world and Maddie a year older.

"You ready for the game Friday night, Tim?" Jake and Tim stopped close to where Liann gathered up the color guard equipment. She figured practice was over for the night, what with the young football player showing up.

"Yep, we're going to crush the Dawgs." Tim smacked his fist into the palm of his other hand. "I'm ready. I know that much."

"I assume you've applied to colleges already?" Jake asked Tim.

Tim opened his mouth, but the front door banged open. "Hey! Just had to freshen up. Ms. Rivers and I were practicing after supper." Maddie stood on the edge of the porch, leaning on one of the supporting poles. Her dark ash-brown hair was sleek and straight, a sky-blue hairband held it back. In the space of barely two minutes, she'd also changed into some dark-blue capris and a white blouse with a wide, ruffled neckline.

"Hi, Maddie." Tim wiped his palms on his pants legs.

"Hi there." Maddie sauntered down to ground level. "Tim, this is Ms. Rivers. She's my coach. I can't wait until opening game. I just wish you could see us perform."

"Probably can't." The boy glanced at Jake then relaxed. "We'll be celebrating being ahead at halftime."

"That's the way to think about it," Jake said. "You two are working very hard this season. I'm proud of both of you."

Maddie beamed at Tim, who returned her look. Oh, boy. Liann would definitely pray for Jake then warn him. He was going to have his hands full this fall.

&

Jake stepped out onto the turf of Yellowjackets Stadium. The stadium's lights glowed, even though sunset was still more than an hour away. Time for kickoff in thirty minutes.

There was nothing like the first home game of the season. The atmosphere crackled with energy as the metal bleachers filled with fans wearing yellow shirts. Restaurants in Starlight might as well shut down during the football game, because the crowd gathered here tonight. The familiar, heady rush of Texas football hit Jake as he scanned the turf stretching one hundred yards in the other direction.

And a twinge of nerves, too. Somewhere in the stands sat a coaching representative from Kansas Tech.

"You about ready?" Coach Blann, twenty-five years his elder, had been a fixture in Yellowjackets football for nearly two decades.

"Yes, sir." The boys were back in the locker room, whooping it up, tying their cleats, straightening their pads, and waiting for their pep talk and a quick prayer before heading onto the field. They'd enter with a cloud of smoke and the crack of a cannon.

"We're going to have a great season. Best ever." Blann's gaze roamed the bleachers.

"I'm ready for us to stomp on some Dawgs tonight," Jake said. He didn't think about losing, or falling back. Every play sealed up nice and neat, every pass caught. No one would sack Tim Rollins, either. The kid was by far the best quarterback they'd had in recent years and was up for his final season. If he kept improving, one day they might even watch him on the NFL.

"Listen, Tucker." Blann strode along the sideline to the nearest of three long yellow plastic benches where the team sat when they weren't striving to gain yardage. "I haven't made any official announcement yet, but I turned in my paperwork to the district this week. This will officially be my last season."

"We'll miss you, sir. You've made some great contributions to this organization."

"I wanted to let you know that I'm recommending that the superintendent and school board appoint you as my replacement. There'll be red tape and proper paperwork to file, but you're my top pick. They'll bat around some names for show, but in the end, I want the job to go to you. You've earned it. You've been a mentor to these boys, and I know they'll respond to you." Blann held up his hand. "I know Kansas is here tonight, and I'm mighty proud of that. But I can't think of anyone else better suited to be head coach of the 'Jackets.'"

"I—I'm honored." Jake couldn't say anything else. He'd be the youngest head coach in the history of Starlight football. This year he planned to keep the state championship in his sights, and he wouldn't let the team forget it, either.

"So, think about it. Before you start packing for Kansas and that junior assistant coach position you want." Blann turned and faced the cinder-block structure at the end of the field that housed the locker rooms. "Those boys look up to you. They'll listen to you without giving you much grief. You're a symbol of hope to them, that they can put those skills they learn out here on the field to good use in their lives. Boys like Rollins, the world would say, are a lost cause. Everybody knows his dad spends more time at the local watering hole than at home being a father."

"I don't consider him a lost cause. He's a hard worker, and he'll be ten times the man his father is someday." Jake nodded. "Thank you, Coach." The other night, he'd been glad to see Tim stop by the house. Even if the boy was using it as an excuse to see Maddie, it was yet another chance for Jake to be a positive influence on him. But though Jake wasn't going to consider staying in Starlight, he wasn't going to tell Blann that just yet. And at least when he left, it wouldn't be a surprise.

The band was starting to file in and arrive, and he spotted Maddie and Liann with the color guard squad. Liann wore simple black track pants topped by a Yellowjackets shirt, but Maddie wore her full uniform—white leggings covered with a simple, flowing yellow skirt. *Just like Belle's in the movie*, Maddie had said.

One of the drummers on the line started beating on a bass drum, and the sound set the Yellowjackets fans into a frenzy, humming on their kazoos. The sound almost made Jake laugh every time he heard it—an incessant buzzing that mingled with the cheers. He figured that was as threatening as a Yellowjacket could sound. Considering they were playing the Copperas Cove Bulldawgs tonight, they needed all the buzz they could get.

Maddie waved at him from across the field and tugged on Liann's arm. Liann gave a single wave then turned her focus back to directing the girls, pointing to where they should place their equipment.

The memory of Saturday night had followed Jake all through the week. Part of him wanted to ask Liann out on a real date, but he knew it wouldn't be fair to her. Plus, she'd been engaged very recently. He wasn't about to be her consolation prize. So here they were. Also, there was the Kansas Tech recruiter in the stands, holding binoculars.

Now the cheerleaders ran the length of the home side, waving and doing their backflips. Jake had warned the boys not to be distracted by the girls in black and yellow. They were there to focus on the game. Tonight was for winning, not finding a girlfriend. The game would help them better themselves. When those on either squad started intermingling, distractions could cost them games. Too many lost games could cost someone their future. Every decision could have lifelong consequences.

Blann had crossed to where the trainers were setting up the water stations for the home team and was bawling somebody out for something. He respected Blann, but sometimes the man was overly picky. He said he was "old school," but Jake didn't like how he talked about women as if they weren't quite equal to men. That didn't set right with Jake. Maddie had told him once that Coach Blann had yelled at her for putting the water cooler on the wrong end of the bench.

Jake knew if he were head coach around here, things would change. Not the standard of excellence that Blann promoted, but the politics of athletics. Jake wouldn't play that kind of game. He sucked in a deep breath, blew it out, then looked at his watch. Time to head back to the locker room.

He left the field, crossed a small expanse of lawn, and entered the long narrow building. Shouts and locker doors slamming masked the sounds of someone's iPod.

Jake whistled through his fingers and banged on the nearest locker with his fist. "Listen up, y'all!" The voices fell silent, and someone turned off the music. "We're about ready to go. The Dawgs are tough, but they haven't felt the Yellowjackets sting!" The boys roared in response. Jake felt the eyes of the kings of Starlight's gridiron on him.

Coach Blann stepped forward. "Boys, let's take a knee b'fore we head out."

The boys in their black and yellow jerseys each sank to the floor on one knee, their helmets clutched in one hand.

"Let's bow our heads."

Jake felt the hush sweep through the locker room. Sure, they prayed before the games. It was tradition. It was Texas football. He didn't know what all the boys believed, but he always prayed they sensed God's presence in that room, that Someone much bigger than them took joy in their sportsmanship.

He remembered a moment during his senior year when an ordinary game turned into one that changed his life and firmly cemented his childhood faith. When he bowed his head as the captain prayed, he felt God's presence, and knew God was with him in Starlight. Everything would be okay. The memory made his throat catch even now as they waited for Coach Blann to pray. God, with him in Starlight... But that didn't mean he was supposed to stay, because God was in Kansas, too.

Coach Blann glanced around before bowing his head. "Heavenly Father, we thank You for tonight. Help us to play hard, play fair, play tough. Help us to be at the top of our game. Protect us and the Dawgs from harm. Let us remember to give You the glory for everything You have given us. In Your Son's name we pray, amen."

"Amen!" The boys rose up and started clapping each other's backs and fastening helmets.

"Coach Tucker, talk to us." Coach Blann looked at him. The clock was ticking closer to seven thirty and kickoff.

Jake cleared his throat. "This is our first game of the season, but you play like it's your last game. You seniors are looking ahead to graduation. You're not graduating tonight. Some of you are thinking of that girl who'll be waiting for you after the game. You're not getting married tonight. You're not cleaning your room or mowing your lawn. Tonight's not about homework or the television show you're missing. Tonight, you are Yellowjackets. If you were to walk off the field tonight and never go back on, what are you going to leave behind you?" The hum from the overhead lights accented his words. The undertones of the bass drums outside and the faint roar from the stands drifted through the windows near the ceiling. "Be all in tonight. Be here tonight. Be the kind of player that those younger boys out there should be watching." He nodded at Coach Blann.

"Let's go sting some Dawgs!" Blann growled.

Jake had more flickers of memory from more than ten years ago, going out there in the same uniform. The years had flown, and Coach Blann had turned from his coach into his colleague. Jake and Coach Blann and the rest of the staff followed the team to the waiting area.

The cheers and screams rose up as the team waited inside the inflated black-and-yellow striped tunnel, with a paper barrier blocking them from the field ahead.

"And now let's call this fall's team out onto the field—the Starrrrlight Yellowjacketsssss!" The team tore through the paper barrier and spilled out of the tunnel. Jake brought up the rear with the rest of the coaching staff and trainers as they ran the gauntlet of cheerleaders and the performance dance troupe, the Honeybees.

He blocked everything else out—the buzz of the kazoos, the clicking of the telephoto lenses, the band playing the "Anthem to Starlight" that everyone knew by heart. Even the knowledge that Liann sat with her squad in the bleachers next to the band. Tonight was for Tim and the rest of the boys of Starlight.

Then came the national anthem and the school's anthem. He couldn't believe he'd been in those boys' cleats not so long ago. So much had changed for him since then, but the surroundings remained the same.

A Kansas Tech ball cap at the edge of the stands caught his eyes. "C'mon boys," he said to no one in particular. "Let's show 'em what we've got."

eight

"People are staring," Liann said as she and Aunt Chin Mae walked into The Pit for breakfast on Saturday morning.

"Of course they stare. You do something that no one has done in many years." Her aunt smiled as she waved across the restaurant to an older woman with copper-red hair, sitting in a booth. "Even though the Yellowjackets lose to those Dawgs last night, we hold our heads high because of the band show. The Starlight band just as good as the Pride of Cove, who always wins the Central Texas marching contest."

Liann studied the faces in the room to see if anyone looked familiar. Starlight's barbecue hot spot opened for down-home country breakfasts. Liann was sure she'd need to work out double time to keep her arteries from clogging if she ate here too often. Framed autographed photographs of celebrities lined the wall behind the register. Elvis Presley was one of them, wearing an army uniform from the time he was stationed nearby at what was once Camp Hood.

She yawned. She'd never forget last night. The band and color guard's halftime performance had shoved the crowd into a cheering frenzy that carried into the second half, but the excitement was not enough to spur the Yellowjackets on to a win. She and the girls, however, had flown on a giddy enthusiasm as a result of their role in the halftime show. Maddie had been brilliant with her rifle skills, even though she dropped her flag once during the opening movement.

Last night's loss had to have hurt Jake. Liann scanned the booths and tables. Maybe he stayed home to figure out what went wrong. But if he were here, she'd tell him not to blame himself. Sometimes, you just had a bad night.

Aunt Chin Mae led her over to the redheaded lady. "Azalea, I got Ms. Sleepy-Do to join us."

"Hey, it's been a long week." Liann laughed.

"Hi, I'm Azalea Bush," the redhead said. "You've met my husband, Herb, already."

"Liann Rivers."

"So you're the sweet young lady I've been hearing all about." Azalea smiled warmly, her blue eyes sparkling. "We hope you love Starlight and plan to stay here a long time."

"I'm not sure how long I'll be here. At least for this fall."

"She dumped her fiancé." Aunt Chin Mae clucked her tongue. "Just in time, too. So she come here, and I'm glad. She has a new boyfriend now."

Liann shook her head. "No, not exactly." Not if he was chasing a dream of coaching a Big Twelve team—a dream that would take him away from Starlight.

"Anyway, you ought to meet Tamarind Brown." Azalea glanced across the room. "Tam! Hey, come meet someone."

A lanky brunette with long curly hair and light, cinnamon-toned skin said a few words to one table's occupants then ambled toward them. "Hey, Aunt Zalea."

"Tamarind, this is Liann Rivers, Chin Mae's niece." Azalea gestured to Liann. "She teaches the high school color guard. Just moved here."

"Well, I'm really glad to meet you." Tamarind's green eyes were vivid in her tawny face. "I heard that was an awesome halftime show last night. Wish I hadn't missed it."

"Thanks. And it's nice to meet you, too."

"Tam!" a voice called from the kitchen.

"Hang on," Tamarind called over her shoulder. "I need to run. You two want coffee?"

Liann nodded. "Sounds great to me."

"I'll send some over." Tamarind sped off toward the kitchen, Azalea watching her.

"Sweet, sweet girl." Azalea sighed. "We need to find someone for her, especially after what happened with Billy. But she's so gun-shy. She's a good girl, too. Goes to church and knows her Jesus. Doesn't go hitting the nightclubs looking for a soldier."

"What happened with Billy?" The words flew from Liann's mouth. Here she sat, with two of the town's biddies, and she was letting them assimilate her into their problem-solving club.

"Oh. . . Let's just say it wasn't meant to be between them. I know she wanted it to be, though." Another sigh from Azalea.

"She's going away soon," said Aunt Chin Mae. "Culinary school. I think she's going to come back here and buy The Pit. Her parents are helping her."

"Good for her," said Azalea.

"Coffees?" A waitress stopped at the table with two steaming mugs.

"Right here." Aunt Chin Mae tapped the table in front of her, and the waitress set the mugs down. "Now, Liann. What about you? Did you work things out with Jake?"

Liann found the cream and doctored her coffee. "No, but there's nothing to work out, really. I do like him, but he has his goals, and I have mine. I don't think they're the same."

"Give it time, hon," Azalea said, patting her hand. "Those Tucker boys make up their minds, and there's nothing changing it except an act of God. So let God do His thing."

"That sounds great to me. I'm going to keep busy with work." She had the feeling if she sat here long enough, the two older women would figure out the rest of her life for her, too. Sweet ladies. But she'd had enough of other people thinking they knew what was best for her.

"Who's *that*?" Azalea stared toward The Pit's entryway. "He definitely ain't from around here."

Liann and Aunt Chin Mae looked in the direction of Azalea's stare. A male figure, backlit by the sun. He lifted an arm to his face, pulling off a pair of sunglasses. *Matt?* Liann ducked lower onto the cushioned seat, trying to use her aunt's body to block his view of her.

❧

Jake cast the fishing line into the center of the river, and the loose line drifted on the breeze. He had enough shade from here in the late morning sun before it disappeared. His visit with Liann to the river last Saturday reminded him of how much he enjoyed fishing. A man could do a lot of thinking while waiting for a bite. Or no thinking at all.

The Kansas coaching scout never made it down to the field, and Jake's phone didn't ring, either. Of course, last night's loss still dug into him, and that pain and aggravation overshadowed any disappointment over what didn't happen with the scout.

What was he expecting, a job offer that evening? Was he prepared to walk out on the team so early in the season? And then, there were Coach Blann's words to him.

Top coaching spot in Starlight. He'd prayed about that

last night. He had to, like any major decision. He continued the conversation now. "Lord, You know how much I want to coach college ball. To work at that level, even as an assistant coach."

Some people wondered why he wasn't a teacher or even a preacher. A few of the others on the coaching staff called him "Preacher Jake," and that was fine by him. No, he didn't feel that calling on his life.

He heard a vehicle coming toward the end of the trail. As the noise grew louder, he turned to see a late-model sedan approaching at a crawl. Tim Rollins. He parked the car and ambled in his direction.

"Maddie said you were down here. I tried calling but got your voice mail."

"Turned my phone off." Jake turned back to the river, feeling a tug on his line before it went slack again. Either it was a branch, or something was playing with the bait.

"Sorry about the game. The Dawgs are tough." Tim stood at the end of the trail.

"We knew it would be a tough fight. The Dawgs have made the playoffs and the state finals several times over the last few years." He tugged on the line. "We'll go out there and attack it on Monday morning. Shake it off. They outplayed us last night. We'll look at the films and figure out how they did it."

Tim had the fidgets. "Yeah. We'll do better next Friday."

"You won't just do better. You'll win. Go out there expecting to win. Don't expect it to be easy. Ever." He eyeballed the boy, who flinched as if he were under an interrogation lamp. "So, what brings you here? You never come out to talk about the game."

"I, uh. . . I was wondering if I could take Maddie to the play tonight at the high school."

"What's playing?" Oh, wow. He'd never contemplated this when he agreed to keep an eye on Maddie.

"*Into the Woods*. A comedy. There's a visiting drama group coming for a performance." Tim rested a hand on his belt buckle. "Then I wanted to take her to Dairy Queen. My friend Kyle Sanders is going, too, with his girlfriend, so we'll be in a group."

"You don't say." A good thing, four of them going together. Another thought tickled his brain. "I thought you were seeing Cassandra, on the cheer squad."

"We broke up over the summer. Too much drama for me."

"I see." Jake let the silence stretch out like a strand of mozzarella cheese. He had to give Tim credit for showing up here at all. "You spend any amount of time with a teenage girl, you're going to get drama. How do I know the same won't happen with Maddie?"

"She's different."

Jake chuckled. "With Maddie, there's never a dull moment. Occasionally some drama. I'm just warning you."

"Well, is it okay if I take her?"

"I need to check with my father to make sure it's all right. But, have her home at ten." Jake gave his best glare.

"The play's at seven."

"Well, if it gets out at nine, that'll give you more than enough time to get some ice cream or a burger and head home again. It's ten, or no deal."

"Understood, Coach." Tim nodded, looked like he was

going to say something else, then trotted back to his car.

Jake set down his fishing pole, picked up his phone, and dialed. "Liann, it's Jake. What are you doing tonight?"

☙

"What am I doing tonight?" Right now, she was melting in the parking lot of The Pit, standing beside Matt and his rental car. "Can I call you back?" Of course, her question probably sent Matt's radar into curiosity mode. Yup, his eyebrows soared upward.

"Sure," Jake said. "It's kind of important."

"All right, then. I'll call you in a few minutes." She ended the call and turned her full attention back to Matt. "I really need to go. It's hot out here, if you didn't notice, and I rode with my aunt." She was going to find out *who* told Matt where she was. Probably her mother, who still lamented that she never got to wear her mother-of-the-bride dress. Liann had already suggested her parents go on a cruise so she could have a chance to wear the gown.

"You're shocked to see me, but I wanted to talk to you in person." Matt looked comfortable but a little out of place in his khakis and button-down shirt, especially on a Starlight Saturday morning.

"I haven't changed my mind, Matt." A vehicle flashed in the sunlight. Aunt Chin Mae's golden bean was negotiating its way around the holes in The Pit's parking lot toward the exit. "No—Aunt Chin Mae!" But knowing her aunt, she probably had her Mozart cranked full blast in the car. And she'd forgotten Liann.

"Looks like you need a ride home." Matt patted the roof of the car. "And we need to talk."

"We can talk here. Really. Plus, I need to make a phone

call soon." She wanted to tear off and chase Aunt Chin Mae down, waving and screaming until her aunt noticed her panicked figure in the rearview mirror.

"What happened to us? I'm still baffled."

"You flew hundreds of miles to ask me this?"

"I'm moving to Texas, Liann. I've applied to several churches looking for youth pastors not far from here. Plus, there's a college outreach program in Austin that needs a director. I thought of you with that one. I understand if you're afraid of being a pastor's wife. Maybe with ministering to students on a college campus, you'll feel less pressure." Matt smiled, and for a few seconds, she remembered why she fell in love with him.

He made her feel as though she were the only person in his world. When he did that, it was easy to go along with almost whatever he proposed. When he *had* proposed marriage, she'd smiled as tears ran down her cheeks and he slipped the one-carat solitaire on her finger. He hadn't asked her what kind of ring she wanted. He'd assumed. She should have seen the signs before then, however.

"You think you know what I want—you've got everything figured out." Liann shook her head. A trail of sweat tickled its way down her back. "I'm not afraid of being a pastor's wife. That's not the issue. I'm not called to do that, I've realized. Yet you make it sound as if you're trying to accommodate me, as if I'm not at your level. Do you realize how patronizing this sounds?"

Matt shook his head and waved her words away. "I'm trying to protect you and think of your needs before mine." Matt took her hand, caressing it in both of his. "Isn't this what you wanted when you used that metaphor of asking me how you liked your eggs cooked?"

"No, it's not." She heard car doors slamming in the parking lot, the crunch of gravel under tires. She pulled her hand free then reached inside her purse. "Don't rearrange your life for me. It's too late for that." She turned and headed back toward the front door of The Pit.

"I'm staying at the HoJo Inn for the weekend, and then I'm heading for Austin. But I'm not giving up on us," Matt called after her.

Liann wanted to believe him, yet the very idea of going back to him made her feel as if a noose were slowly tightening around her neck. She entered the cool restaurant.

Tamarind handed some change to a customer. "Your aunt just left, Liann."

"I know." She tried not to sigh and took her phone from her purse.

"Thanks. See you next time," Tamarind said to the departing customer, who passed Liann and headed out into the heat. She turned to Liann with a frown. "You okay?"

"See that guy out there in the parking lot, the one who came in a while ago?"

"The one who kept staring at you while you ate breakfast?"

"That's the one." Liann squinted out through the glass door. "That's my ex-fiancé."

"He's cute, but him staring like that? Well, that's just a tad creepy." Tamarind moved from behind the counter.

"I really don't want to talk to him anymore, and he won't listen to *no*. I'd rather not call the police. He's more of an annoyance at this point."

"And now you're stranded for the moment, aren't you?"

"Sort of. I was going to call my aunt to come back for me.

I can't believe she left without me. I told her I'd be right back after I finished talking to Matt." Liann raised her hands and shrugged.

"Follow me. He's coming back this way." Tamarind waved her toward the kitchen. "Let me show you where the barbecue pits are. We make the real deal here. You can hang out there for a few while I persuade Mr. Wonderful to go on his merry way."

Liann followed Tamarind through the kitchen with its metal prep tables and walk-in fridge and freezer, past an office with a desk strewn with papers. The aroma of smoke and wood chips grew stronger. Tamarind pulled open a wooden door, and they entered yet another back room.

This one contained two large smokers with chimneys that extended to the ceiling. A closed exit door stood to their left.

"Wait back here for a few minutes and relax. If it gets a little too smoky, you can always duck your head out the back door." Tamarind smiled. "Now, I'll go deal with this guy. You said his name was Matt?"

"That's right."

Tamarind scurried away. Within seconds, Liann's eyes began to water from the smokiness. She had no doubt that The Pit's barbecue was genuine. She pushed through the back door and found herself outside, looking at a plowed-under field that had once grown corn earlier in the season.

Her phone started ringing again. Jake!

"I'm sorry, I meant to call you back," she said.

"That's okay. The reason I called is I'm in a bit of a jam."

"What is it?"

"Tim asked if he could take Maddie to a play at the high school tonight, and I agreed. I talked to my dad, and he said it was fine, as long as they visited public places in small groups. So they're not going alone. Two other kids will be there. I told him they could go to Dairy Queen, too, but to be home by ten."

"So how does this mean you're in a jam?"

"I'm going to the play, too. I want to make sure she'll be all right. Tim's a good kid. He's in the youth group at Starlight Community Church, but that's no guarantee of anything."

"That's true." She could tell him stories of things she'd encountered while supporting Matt's ministry in the youth group in California. "How can I help you out of this jam you're in?"

"Come with me to the play. I don't want to go alone. My treat at Dairy Queen, too." He paused for a moment. "Don't worry, it's not really a date. I mean. . ."

For the second time ever, he stammered again. She decided to rescue him before he made it sound worse. "Of course we can go as friends. That's perfectly fine with me. No pressure."

"I'll pick you up at six thirty, then. You can dress casual, too. We don't get too fancy with the plays at the school."

"See you later." She ended the call and watched a bird soar over the field then swoop down, probably on a mouse. She never imagined that she'd feel like that little mouse where Matt was concerned. Yet here she was, running to Jake. Sure, he'd called her. But it was so easy for her to say yes. . .

"Okay, he's gone." Tamarind entered the barbecue shack, wiping her hands on a dishcloth. "I told him to buzz off. When someone said no, they meant no. And if I needed to, I'd call the cops."

"Well, thank you so much. But like I said, he's not dangerous or anything. He's a youth pastor." Liann almost wished she'd seen Matt's face when Tamarind asked him to leave.

"My point exactly," said Tamarind. "You should see the relief all over your face."

nine

The lights of Hattie Hempstead Auditorium grew dim, and the stage looked far away from Liann and Jake's vantage point. A colorful set created a woodland setting for the junior-senior play. But Jake focused on four young people in the eighth row to the far right of the stage.

"So far, he hasn't tried anything." Jake tried to keep his voice low as he leaned toward Liann.

"What if he does? What are you going to do?" Liann flipped through her program and held it up in the dim light. "March down there and pull them apart?"

"If I have to, I will." Truthfully, he didn't know. He tried to think about his own high school years. He'd been busy with the team, and the girls seemed petty, catty, and not worth the hassle. Maybe he'd dodged plenty of bullets all those years. Moving around when they were kids, though, always made him and Billy hit the popular list in school. Billy brooded more, which also boosted his mystique with the girls. They seemed to like the mysterious type. Jake was just trying to get through school so he could move on to the big time.

Tim had appeared at 6:25 p.m., which was just in time if Jake was going to pick up Liann. As it was, Maddie had wanted to pause in the entryway to get their photo together. It scared Jake to see his sister as a young woman. If he ever had daughters, he'd resolve to lock them in a box until they were twenty-five, at least.

The play started, and his eyelids grew heavy. He blinked to see Tim whisper something in Maddie's ear. Then Maddie nodded and glanced over her shoulder. Jake bent as if to tie his shoe. As he did so, Liann reached down for her purse. Their heads nearly cracked together. Her perfume was a little flowery, with a hint of spice that kept it from being too sweet. Just like her. Why did women *do* things like wear that kind of perfume? She pushed a button on her cell phone, and it went dark.

Jake straightened up. Good. Maddie must not have seen him. When intermission came, however, she probably would. Maybe she'd make more of a deal out of him being out with Liann, which was fine by him.

His eyelids felt heavier, so he decided to close them for a few minutes. He wasn't much of a theater guy. He heard Liann chuckle at some of the lines. What a pretty laugh she had. But then, she *was* pretty. . .

Someone was poking his side. "The gig's up, Coach." Liann.

Jake sat up in the auditorium seat, blinking. The lights were at full strength again. He blinked at Liann. "I was only out for a few minutes. . . ."

"Right." She poked him again in the ribs. "You snorted once. I had to cough to cover it up."

He looked toward Maddie and Tim's seats but didn't see his sister. Tim still sat there, next to Kyle Sanders from the team, and the two boys were talking. "When did Maddie leave?"

"As soon as the lights came up, she and the other girl left down the other aisle." Liann glanced toward the doors in the rear corner of the auditorium. "She knows we're here. She waved at me and started giggling when she saw you with your head tilted back."

"Did she look mad?"

"No. Surprised, but not mad."

Chatting female voices grew louder. "Hey, so what are y'all doing here?" Maddie stood at the end of the row, her hands on her hips. "You don't even like plays." She glared at him.

"I. . .um. . ." Jake's brain fumbled then dropped his thought.

"He invited me." Liann began.

"I wanted to make sure you were okay," he blurted.

"You're not Dad." Maddie frowned.

"I know, but I told him I'd watch out for you."

"You're there all day at school, and you don't see me." Maddie crossed her arms over her chest. "How do you know I'm not getting into trouble there?"

"I don't think you get into trouble at school."

"Well then, why can't I go out with Tim, plus Kyle, plus Bekah, without having my chaperones hovering in the back?" Maddie shot a look at Liann.

"Watch your tone, Madelynn. I'm not your dad, yes. But he asked that I watch out for you. We don't want anything to happen to you."

Maddie lowered her arms, and her shoulders drooped. "I know. I'm sorry. But I'm careful. Tim's sweet and funny. He got accepted at TSU, did you hear? He just found out today."

"No, I didn't know."

"See, he's a lot like you. Going to your alma mater. He's like Dad, too. He's a hard worker. He wants to be a teacher, too." Maddie glanced from him to Liann then back to him again. "Were you planning on going to Dairy Queen after the play?"

Jake nodded.

"That figures." But she smiled at him as she returned to her seat.

❧

A line of cars snaked its way to the drive-through window at Dairy Queen. Liann studied the menu. She remembered coming here as a kid when her aunt and uncle would take her out for an ice-cream treat.

"I'm getting something a little more substantial than ice cream." Jake patted his stomach. "Maybe a burger and fries, and some ice cream. So order whatever you want."

"I think I'll just have a Blizzard." She looked at the line of vehicles. Tim's car was three ahead of them. "I figured the kids were going to eat inside."

Jake frowned. "I did, too. I also thought the drive-through would be a faster way to get our food. He'd better not be driving out to the ridge." He drove out of their place in line and found an empty space at the end of the lot. They left his truck and headed to the restaurant.

"Liann."

She glanced to her right and saw Matt standing beside his parked car. She tried not to gasp, but now she felt like he *was* following her. She tried not to shiver. "What are you doing here?"

Jake stopped and turned to face Matt. "Can we help you with something?"

"That's my fiancée you've taken on a date tonight. First a play, and now dessert?"

Liann shook her head. "Matt, I'm not your fiancée anymore. What were you doing, following us?"

"You've moved on awfully fast." Matt took a step closer. "Is this what you had planned all along? Turn me in for someone new? Three months ago you were willing to spend the rest of your life with me."

"Look," Jake said, taking a step in Matt's direction, "Liann's life is her business. If she believes you're not the one for her, you should be thanking God she came to that decision before you exchanged vows."

"I'm moving here, because of you—" Matt began.

"He's moving *here*?" Jake stared at Liann.

"Austin, actually," said Matt. "Close enough to see you. Close enough to work on our relationship."

Liann clutched Jake's arm for support. Unbelievable. How could she have been so blind? *Thank You, Lord, for helping me avoid this disaster.* "Matt, I only want to be friends with you. Friends only. Nothing more."

"But we prayed. We believed this was God's will." Matt rubbed his hair. "What changed? I don't believe God changes His mind."

Liann wanted to grab Jake's keys and make a run for his truck then disappear somewhere, anywhere. Any old road that led out of Starlight, away from Matt. But she stood firm. "I was wrong, and I realized it. That's what changed. It's me."

"You listened to fear. Fear erodes our faith—in God, in the ones we love."

Liann sensed movement nearby. A few people stood outside the Dairy Queen, watching them. Great. Drama in a small town, and she'd brought it with her from California. "We're done, Matt. All the spiritualizing won't change my mind. C'mon, Jake. I think I'll get a burger, too."

A vehicle rolled past. There went Tim and Maddie. Liann had no idea what time it was. She glanced up at Jake.

"I lost my appetite. Let's get out of here," he said. He took her hand, and they turned and jogged back to his truck. She didn't look back at Matt—she couldn't. Part of what he said made sense. She'd allowed herself to move awfully fast with Jake, just like she had with Matt.

He opened her door and helped her inside the truck. She climbed into the cab, her stomach roiling. Maybe it was a good thing they needed to skip the Dairy Queen and chase off after Maddie.

Soon they roared out under the moonlight. "When did this 'Matt' arrive in town?"

"This morning. He told me he's applied for youth pastor positions in Austin and also for a campus ministry position at a college." She watched out the window as they passed the downtown buildings of Starlight's square.

"That's no coincidence." He braked the truck, and they stopped at a traffic light, waiting as no one passed through the intersection.

"No." She glanced at him. "But I'm not changing my mind. I had to make a break for a good reason. My mother doesn't understand. She thinks there's nothing wrong with Matt, that he's absolutely perfect. Maybe in some ways, but not for me."

"He seems stubborn. That's definitely *not* one of the fruits of the Spirit, and not one of the qualities of love. Remember, 'Love doesn't insist on having its own way,' says one version." He gave her a smile, and she caught her breath. She turned her face to the window again. There went her heart. But then, he was so bent on leaving. . . Her mind began to race.

God wasn't the author of confusion. The scriptures told her that. Right now, though, she didn't feel confused. No, she wasn't going back to Matt. Of that, she was certain. But Jake? She found herself going along with things now, going with the flow tonight. How long was it before she started feeling like she did with Matt? She didn't want to go down that road again. Matt didn't deserve it.

Neither did Jake.

ten

Liann buried herself in work for the next two weeks. She had color guard during the day, football games on Friday nights, and bee-keeping with Uncle Bert or Aunt Chin Mae on free nights and on Saturdays. Matt didn't call, didn't e-mail either. She didn't know if he was still pursuing employment in Austin. Also, it was easy enough—or hard enough—to avoid Jake. The band kept rehearsing in the parking lot with the color guard, and if she let herself, she could keep herself from spotting Jake among the coaching staff with their matching shirts.

Saturday came, and after covering her two-mile run, she cooled off and headed for the beehives. The season was dwindling, and Uncle Bert said after the fall harvest from his garden, the bees would have less pollen to use.

Aunt Chin Mae waved. "Finally, you here! Come help." She had a harvester contraption next to the hive. "It's too heavy for me."

Liann pulled on her gloves, stepping closer to the hive. She felt like an old pro now, her heartbeat steady and breathing rate normal around the swarming critters. Amazing, how the bees created honey from the pollen. They kept the honey in the brood box for themselves, but anything in the stacked super boxes above was free for the humans.

"Ah, good." Her aunt smiled beneath her veiled hood. "We'll get plenty of jars from this one alone."

Liann had been stung—several times—since helping her aunt with the bees, and she took the pain in stride. Not that she'd grown used to it, but it came with caring for the insects.

"You been quiet since that Matt left town." Aunt Chin Mae cleaned the inner feeder of one of the hives.

"I've been busy. The team is working hard."

"Yes, but you don't look as happy."

"Sometimes, I wish I were a bee." Liann sighed and held the super box steady for her aunt. "More smoke?"

"Yes. Right there at the top."

Liann reached for the smoker and sent gray puffs into the top of the box. The bees, soothed by the smoke, settled into the lower levels.

"Why do you sometimes wish to be a bee?"

"They know exactly what they're supposed to do—the queen, the workers, the drones. God designed them for their purpose, and they instinctively know. We humans have it so much more complicated." Liann had received an e-mail from Beth:

If Matt's in Texas, you should come back. I hear that Ventura High will be looking for a replacement coach after the first of the year. Don't let one bad experience hold you back from all that God still has for you.

Was this an open door, showing her that she belonged back in California? She didn't know.

"I think we complicate things on our own." Aunt Chin Mae pulled the next frame from the hive. "You made a mistake with Matt. You gave up everything you wanted for him, gave up who you are. We give up things for people we love, but we should never give up who we are."

"You and my mother both married American brothers." Liann wanted to sneak a taste of the fresh honey but decided to wait until later. "You barely knew English, but you came here from Korea anyway. Did you feel like you gave up everything for Uncle Bert?"

"Not at all. I am Korean, but I am American. It's my country now, for many years. I say yes to Bert, I say yes to life here as his wife. But he did not want me to leave my Korea behind. So, your mother and I keep traditions that the younger ones, like you, don't remember or don't know." Her aunt straightened then stretched her back. "It was different here for me, but I knew other women had done the same. I love Bert. He is a good Christian man who still loved me even though I could not have children. Unconditional love, he gives me."

Liann's eyes stung. "I'm glad he did. My mother feels the same way about Dad."

"And I'm so glad she was able to give him you, and then loan you to us."

"Aw, Aunt Chin Mae. . ."

"Having you around is almost like having a daughter. That's why I worry about you. I want you happy, married, not so sad."

"I want to be happy without being married."

"What about today? You happy today?"

Liann paused. The morning sun wasn't quite as hot as it was when she first arrived in late July. Labor Day weekend was upon them. Last night, the girls had done an outstanding job. She had a good roof over her head, and now she was enjoying time with her aunt, something she'd done as a child but, she realized, meant more now as an adult.

"Yes, I am. I have a lot of blessings, even without a man in my life." She missed Jake, but it was better this way. He'd sort of buried himself in work, too. However, football season claimed many a man's attention in Starlight. Lord willing, they'd busy themselves into the playoffs.

A blaring car horn made both of them jump. A vaguely familiar-looking sedan came up the driveway. Maddie negotiated the car to park beside Trixie, still out of commission. Biff had said it was the transmission. Liann remembered the one thing that did *not* make her happy today: not having enough money to fix Trixie. She'd had to get rides to school from Uncle Bert on his way in for breakfast at The Pit to chew the fat along with the other veterans of his era.

Maddie left the car and trotted over toward the hives, not seeming to mind the bees. "Ms. Rivers, I need your help." She stopped at a respectful distance. "I don't know who else to turn to right now. My Aunt Justine is gone, filming her show. She doesn't get back until Homecoming night, and the dance is the day after."

"What is it?" Liann glanced at Aunt Chin Mae, who waved her off to join Maddie. She peeled her gloves from her sweaty hands and forearms.

"Homecoming!" Maddie blurted out the word as if that should explain everything.

"Yes, that's two weeks from Saturday." Liann ought to know. She thought of the extra money she was going to make for chaperoning the Homecoming dance. What she hadn't thought of was her own dress. Not that the dress mattered, or whether she had room for such a purchase in her budget.

"I know. Tim asked me to be his date, and I need a dress."

"So what about Jake, or Billy?"

Maddie shook her head. "*Really*, Ms. Rivers? My older brothers are pretty smart, but they're clueless about fashion. Especially for something this important."

"Okay. Maybe we can go to Killeen one evening."

"Well, I was hoping we could go to Austin next Saturday."

Liann tried not to grin. "You sound like you had this already planned."

"I had to have something figured out." Then her face lost its glow. "Look, I'm not sure what happened between you and my brother the night of the play, but he hasn't been the same."

"Maddie, you're sweet to ask, but don't worry. He and I are okay." Liann didn't want to overstep in the teacher-pupil relationship. She had begun to think of Maddie almost like a niece, or a little sister even, but she didn't want to tell the young lady more. However, even if Maddie wasn't her student, she didn't know what to say.

❧

One hour after driving down Route 183, Jake pulled off the highway at Austin's Lakeline Plaza. He'd ended up as driver by default. Billy was out of town with Justine, so that left Jake to play chauffeur since Maddie's driving skills were not up to driving in the city. He yawned as he checked the mirror and merged onto the access road. So here he was, with the fog of last night's game still hanging in his brain. They'd won—barely—in the last few minutes of the fourth quarter, with a perfect pass from Tim to one of the receivers.

"Okay, Jake, I have a list." Maddie flashed a white piece of paper in his periphery.

"Don't look so surprised," Liann said beside him, a warm chuckle punctuating her comment.

"How many places do you think it'll take to find one dress?" Jake shook his head. "We're planning to start at the mall first, right?"

"We might find the perfect dress right away. You never know. Right, Ms. Rivers?"

"It's true, Jake. Guys have it so much easier finding the right clothes."

"I think you women just make it harder than it needs to be." He glanced at Liann. He tried not to keep his focus off the road for too long, but seeing her smile up close made him realize how much he'd missed her.

"No, we don't." She started ticking off items on her finger, one by one. "There's color, and hemline, and how the waist is fitted, and the neckline. Then there are sleeves—long, short, sleeveless, spaghetti straps—"

"—and strapless!" Maddie called from over his shoulder.

"No!" both he and Liann said simultaneously.

Liann grinned at them both and continued. "Plus there's fabric—pattern, texture, weight. And last but not least, what hides figure flaws the best. If we're going to wear a wrap, or a shrug. Although, Maddie, I think you'll look beautiful in almost anything we find for you."

"My thighs are too fat." Maddie slapped her legs.

"I don't think so," said Liann. "You have classic proportions. I think you're just right for your age."

Maddie sighed. "One of the cheerleaders said the color guard all have thunder thighs."

"What?" Liann turned to look at Maddie. "To your faces?"

"No. Someone else heard them say it." Maddie frowned.

"Well, I'll have a talk with Coach Stevens." Liann's dark eyes snapped in Jake's direction.

"You'll always find mean girls throughout life," Jake said. He'd heard trash-talking among some of the football players. Half of it was the boys joking, half rooster crowing to look cool. He usually reminded them that they needed to show how good they were instead of putting someone else down. Girls, though, had a particular acidity to their personalities sometimes. It bewildered him, hearing caustic words coming from sweet-looking creatures.

"True. But someone needs to tell them how damaging words can be." Liann frowned. "I know they don't care, but it's the principle of the thing."

"No—Ms. Rivers. Don't say anything. I don't want it to seem like I'm tattling. And everyone will figure out it's me who told."

"How will they know that?"

"Because everyone knows how. . .close. . .you are with our family."

Jake glanced in the rearview mirror then back at the road that led to the mall. People had noticed. Of course they did. It would be hard to miss. The school play, the odd confrontation with Matt outside Dairy Queen.

After they made it into the first store, a place called Spice, Sugar, and Sass, Jake found himself surrounded by racks of frothy fabric, sequins, and a few dresses he would definitely *not* let his little sister wear. Maddie and Liann went round and round the store until they'd collected six possibilities. Maddie had some definite preferences, but Liann wasn't swayed.

"No, Maddie, the sheath dress won't make you look

thinner because it's tighter. You won't be able to walk or sit comfortably." Liann looked at Jake over the top of the clothing racks.

"It has a slit." Maddie had her hand clamped on the hanger.

"You don't need a slit," Liann responded, much to Jake's relief. The sheath went back to the display rack. "Try these on." A saleslady led them to a fitting room, and Maddie disappeared inside.

Jake leaned closer to Liann. "I owe you. Big-time. I could have *never* done this alone."

"I'm sure you would have done fine."

"No, probably not. She's persistent, and today I'm exhausted. It wouldn't have been pretty."

Liann sank onto a nearby cushioned bench, and he joined her. "Why don't you tell your parents it might be better if Maddie lived with them? They *are* her parents. You and Billy moved around, and you both turned out great. Why's Maddie the exception? She wouldn't be the first kid to start at a new high school." She tried to keep her voice low.

"They wanted to give her as stable a life as possible. It wasn't easy, moving as much as we did. Then when we ended up at Fort Hood, Maddie was a toddler, and they'd had enough of moving the family. She's the only one of us who's been to school in just one town."

"But she still needs her parents. I know it's a hard age. And girls are under so much pressure—"

"Okay, the first dress is on." Maddie exited the dressing room and walked a small circle in front of a set of full-length mirrors.

"You look like you're floating." Liann clapped her hands

together. "It's beautiful. Almost like someone from *Phantom of the Opera*, except without the long skirt."

She *did* look beautiful. The dress was ladylike but wasn't stuffy. It showed off her slim waist, and the soft pink lent a glow to her skin and contrasted with her dark hair.

Jake wondered if Liann had a point, about talking to Mom and Dad and seeing about Maddie finishing school in Colorado. They were trying to protect her from the pain and struggle of being in a new school, being the new one in town.

Hopefully this first dress was *the* dress. "Well, Maddie, is this the one?" he had to ask.

"I don't know. I want to try on these others, just to be sure." She made another pirouette in front of the mirror. Then she paused and looked back at them in the reflection. "Ms. Rivers, what are *you* wearing?"

Liann clutched her hands together around her purse strap. "I haven't decided. I'll wear something, probably one of my church outfits."

"You're working Homecoming?" Jake hadn't known this. He planned to keep an eye on the clock, allowing Maddie and her friends to go out to dinner together—Red Lobster—and then she was going to meet Tim at the house and ride with him to the gymnasium. He thought it a bit strange that Tim wasn't taking her to dinner.

"Yes, we get a one-hundred-dollar stipend for helping out, so I figured, why not?" She bit her lip. "I'm working to earn extra money to get Trixie a new transmission."

"Oh, Ms. Rivers." Maddie stepped forward. "You can't just a regular churchy outfit to Homecoming."

not? I'm just one of the teachers. I don't need to be there in the background to keep order."

"You would definitely *never* fade into the background," Jake said.

Maddie glowed. "If I get the pink dress, it's underbudget. It's on sale. Plus I have an extra twenty-percent-off coupon. That means I still have more money I can spend. Right, Jake?"

❧

Liann swallowed hard. She didn't need to buy a new dress. But the more she thought about it, she *wanted* a new dress. Her budget was nothing like it had been in California. Even with a teacher's salary, she did fine on her own. She had a clothing budget. With her disappointing transition into life in Texas, she'd tossed out purchasing items like new clothes.

"I like this one," Maddie said, pulling a teal dress from the rack. "What do you think, Jake?"

The poor guy. They'd dragged him, outnumbered, to Austin. Liann feared she'd overstepped when she suggested he ought to talk to his parents about moving Maddie to be with them. Her gut told her trouble brewed, and Jake didn't take the warning seriously. Hopefully she could convince him before an adolescent storm broke.

"Uh, it's. . .nice."

"Maddie, don't put him on the spot like that." Liann laughed and put the dress back. "If that one came in purple, I'd love it." A purple silk day dress that skimmed just below her knees, with short capped sleeves, a V-neck, and ruching at the waist. Definitely a step up from a church dress. Her favorite black platform pumps would match it.

Maddie skimmed her fingers over the rack of dresses. "Oh. In purple. Here it is!" She yanked the hanger from the rack and displayed the dress. "You've got to try it on. Plus clearance."

"I do have some shoes that I could wear with it." Liann picked up the dress and carried it to the nearest changing room. As she slipped on the dress, she heard Jake's low tones with Maddie's higher ones, then a few whispers.

She was down a size, probably from the hectic schedule this fall and from perspiring gallons of water, working in the Texas sun. The dress fit her just right.

A knock sounded on the door. "Ms. Rivers, let us see."

Oh dear. She hadn't thought about *Jake* seeing her in this dress. She should have insisted that, no, she didn't need a dress, that she'd make do. Or sent Jake out of the store, which would be rude.

"Uh, okay." Liann pushed the door open to the fitting room. "Well, here it is. I really like it, a lot. More than I thought it would." She dared not meet Jake's eyes. He was used to seeing her in workout clothes, casual wear, and something a little dressier for church. But nothing like this.

"Ms. Rivers, you're *gorgeous*! Isn't she, Jake?" Maddie's voice had a saucy lilt. Liann figured the young girl was loving this and wondered if she was attempting to play matchmaker. It certainly was convenient that Jake agreed to drive them to Austin.

"Beautiful," Jake said. He cleared his throat and looked at her feet.

"I–I'm going to change back now." Liann darted into the dressing room and got out of the elegant dress and back into her casual clothing. She saw through Maddie's sweet attempt to have her and Jake spend more time together. She gave herself a few seconds to catch her breath.

When she left the dressing room, her new dress in tow, Jake was gone. Maddie still had the pink dress but was looking through the clearance rack.

She glanced up when Liann approached. "Jake got a phone call. He said he'd be right back."

Liann looked past the racks of dresses to the front of the store. Jake pushed a button and strode back in their direction, grinning.

"Ladies, I'm taking you out to dinner to celebrate—that was Kansas on the phone. I'm going to fly up the week after Homecoming to interview." His hazel eyes glowed, the skin at the corners crinkling with his smile.

"Wow, that's great news for you." Liann held the dress like a security blanket. She needed to hang on to her heart, too, because if she didn't, Jake would be toting it with him to Kansas.

eleven

Liann stood in a corner of the high school gymnasium, which provided a perfect vantage point to keep an eye on kids. So far, most of them were behaving. Other chaperones patrolled the halls to make sure no couples were trying to sneak outside. A pair of off-duty police officers was on hand as well.

She saw Maddie a few times, standing with some of the color guard squad. Although the sound man was playing a variety of music, not all the students danced. Liann had never been a fan of dances even in high school, and now she remembered why. She wished she had another way to earn an extra hundred dollars instead of hanging out in a makeshift teen nightclub for three hours.

Most of the students, especially those in the band, recognized her and commented on her dress.

"Your turn for the hallway," said Jessica, the band director. "I didn't see anything or anyone out of the ordinary. Here's a walkie-talkie. Vice Principal Jenkins has the other one. He said to let him know if there are any issues, and he'll alert the police."

"Thanks." Liann accepted the walkie-talkie from Jessica.

"Oh, by the way, I received a phone call from the Ventura, California, school system. They're checking your reference here, making sure everything's all right in Texas. I told them what a fabulous job you've done with the color guard team here and that it would be a shame to lose you to California, but I understood."

"That was fast." One week ago, after returning from the shopping trip with Jake and Maddie, she'd submitted her résumé and an application for the job her former maid of honor had mentioned to her. "Thanks for giving me a good reference."

"I know you were disappointed when you first arrived. I would have been." Jessica smiled. "So I don't blame you for applying somewhere else, if even to test the waters. It's hard to get hired midyear like that, though."

"True, but you're right—I thought I would at least try."

"See you later. You'll meet your replacement back here in about an hour."

"Got it." Liann moved into the hallways in the section facing the front of the school with the lights on full blast. She blinked. A pair of students passed her on their way back from the restrooms. The girls giggled in their short strapless dresses.

Starlight High School had a dress code. However, for some reason that didn't apply for school dances, although Liann thought it wouldn't be a bad idea.

So Jessica had received a call from Ventura. That meant Ventura likely would be calling her, first for a phone interview and then possibly to fly out to California for an in-person interview. She could stay with her parents. They'd love that. Mom would probably try to stuff her with kimchi, especially since Liann had confessed to trying Aunt Chin Mae's and liking it.

And next week Jake would head for Kansas Tech. They'd both be getting what they wanted. She'd get her old type of job back, and Jake's fondest dream would come true, moving up to an NCAA team. That was a big leap for him, but she knew he'd tackle the job just like everything else he did in life.

She didn't know what God had in mind for her, but part of her did miss her family. She could see the color guard through this important fall season and possibly return to California in January. Did she really want to coach cheerleading again? Now that she'd had some distance from the sport, she found her enthusiasm fading. Maybe it was being out of the game for so long, so to speak.

Whispers in the hallway past the restrooms caught her attention. Liann rounded the corner. A dark figure disappeared around the corner at the far end of the hall. A girl with sleek blond hair leaned against the wall, her head bowed, her hand clamped over her mouth, her other arm wrapped around her waist. Her shoulders shook.

Liann quickened her steps. "Hey, what is it?" She placed a hand on the girl's bare shoulder.

"Nothing." But tears streamed down her face.

"Do you need me to call someone for you? Or do you just need a few minutes?" She tried to keep her voice low. "Who was just here? I thought I saw someone going around the corner."

"My. . .friend. They're going back to the dance. I promise. I–I'm not sure what I want to do right now." Her ruined mascara ringed her eyes.

"Hang on, let me get you some tissues." Liann hurried to the restroom, grabbed some paper towels, and dampened a few of them. She returned to the girl.

"Thanks." She dabbed the damp ones on her eyes. "I know

I probably look like a raccoon. Oh, you're Ms. Rivers, the flag coach. I didn't recognize you all dressed up."

"Me neither. What's your name?"

"Cassandra Waters."

Now it was Liann's turn. Cassandra Waters was on the cheer squad. "Oh, okay. Hello. Well, I didn't recognize you either."

"I probably look horrible."

"No. You look upset but not horrible." Liann let the girl alternately keep sniffing and wiping her eyes. "Do you want me to call your mom or someone? Do you have a phone with you?"

"I've got my phone." Cassandra picked up a handbag at her feet and opened it, pulling out a phone. She dialed. "Mom? Can you come get me? No. I can't stay."

"Do you need me to talk to her?"

Cassandra shook her head. "Okay, Mom. I'll be waiting out front." She ended the call then blew her nose with the last remaining paper towel.

"Sorry. The paper towels aren't the best." Liann glanced to the end of the hallway. "Do you need me to walk outside with you? Because you're really not supposed to be in this section of the school."

"No, I can go fine by myself. Thanks, Ms. Rivers."

By the end of the hour, Liann was ready to get back to the gymnasium. Only one more hour before the dance ended. She glanced around the room, which was not quite as crowded as it had been. Evidently some of the kids had lost interest in the dance. She saw a trio of girls from the squad and headed in their direction.

"You girls doing okay?"

They exchanged looks. "Um, yes, we're having a great time. Not that we really wanted to dance much. The chicken dance was fun, though," said Kristen.

"Where's Maddie?"

"Um, I think the bathroom?" Kristen replied.

"I was just there. Didn't see her." Something niggled in the bottom of Liann's gut. Not only was Maddie one of "her" girls, but she'd promised Jake she'd keep an eye on her. "Did she come back in yet?"

A few more looks. "It's about Tim. . . ."

Liann looked across the gymnasium to the far corner that led to the parking lot. Tim Rollins stood talking with Maddie. He leaned closer, extending his hand to the side in a pleading gesture. She shook her head. Tim smacked the concrete wall with the bottom of his fist. Liann moved across the gymnasium, crossing the middle of the makeshift dance floor lit by a glitter ball and kaleidoscope lights.

By the time Liann reached the spot where the couple had stood, Tim was striding away, and Maddie was pushing on the exit door.

"Maddie!" She reached for her shoulder.

The door gave, and Maddie pushed outside. "Ms. Rivers, now's not a good time."

"What's going on?" Liann asked as she followed the teenager into the night. "How can I help you?"

"Nobody can." Maddie stumbled from the sidewalk and onto the parking lot. She kicked off her high heels. "Just. . . please. . .leave me alone."

"Stop, right now. Let me call Jake."

"No!" But Maddie stopped and turned around. "I can't breathe when I'm around him."

"You're not allowed to just go off by yourself. This is school property, and it's a school function. You need a ride home, because it's not safe for you to leave. I can't take you now, because I'm working."

Maddie wiped her eyes. "Call Aunt Justine. She'll come get me. She just got back from her shoot yesterday."

"All right." Within a few minutes, Liann had a ride home lined up for Maddie, who still wouldn't say why she was in tears. Tim, of course.

Liann sighed as she left Maddie at the front of the school. "Maddie, you need to talk to somebody."

"I will. When I'm ready." She sealed her lips shut.

Cassandra from the cheer squad stood ten yards away, her focus on the parking lot and an approaching car. The car stopped at the curb, and Cassandra climbed into the front passenger side. When the car passed Maddie and Liann, Cassandra glared at Maddie and raised her hand in an obscene gesture.

Liann gritted her teeth together. "Maddie, *what* is going on?"

Maddie shook her head and said nothing.

Fine. Liann didn't know what was going on, but one thing was for sure: she was calling Jake as soon as she got back inside the building. They were having a talk about Maddie. *Tonight.*

❧

Starlight only had one twenty-four-hour diner, The Koffee Kup, so that's where Jake said he would meet up with Liann. She'd been vague on the phone, which couldn't be a good thing. Of course, he wouldn't mind seeing her in that knockout purple dress.

He saw Chin Mae's gold car in the parking lot and tucked

his truck into the space beside it. He entered the restaurant and found Liann at the back corner, where it was quiet. She looked a little overdressed in the purple, but he didn't care.

"What's going on?" He slid onto the seat of the booth. She stirred creamer into her coffee, followed by sugar.

"It's Maddie." She sighed.

"Did something happen tonight?" If Tim tried something, the kid wouldn't be allowed past the Tucker Ranch entrance again.

"Yes, as a matter of fact. Did she call you before she left the dance?"

"She did. She told me Justine was picking her up and had invited her to spend the night over there, and we'd meet up at church tomorrow morning."

"I don't know what's wrong. She wouldn't tell me. But it's serious, Jake." Liann's eyes had dark circles under them, but she still looked elegant. "Something's going on with her and Tim and a Cassandra from the cheer squad."

"Oh, boy."

Their waitress appeared. "Coffee, right?"

He nodded. "Black, please."

"Coming right up."

Jake tried not to sigh. "Teenage drama. Tim and Cassandra were an item last school year, but it seems they called it quits over the summer. It happens. High school romances. Not many of them last. He really likes Maddie now, and I'm doing my best to keep an eye on her. As you know."

"Well, I think it's gone beyond a simple high school romance. She was crying tonight after talking to Tim. He looked frustrated, at the very least, before he stormed off. I followed her outside and offered to call you, which she refused. She settled for Justine picking her up."

This time he did sigh. "I'm not surprised. She's been so. . . different. . .this fall. First, changing her courses—not that I blame you for any of this."

"I didn't think you did." She gave him a small smile.

"Then the whole dress thing for Homecoming. Last year, we had to practically drag her to the dress shop here in town to get her something for the Miss Starlight pageant. She wanted to earn a scholarship badly enough to agree to wear an evening gown. This year, she had a shopping strategy all planned out and wanted to make sure she shopped in Austin." Jake shook his head. "And her emotions? She's happy one day, in the dumps the next."

"She's growing up. Those teen-girl emotions are rough." Liann nodded. "Oh, how I remember it well. But this, this is something serious. She's starting to push you away. Me, I wasn't surprised. I'm her teacher and a friend of the family. But when she didn't want me to call you. . ."

"I'm sure she'll be better in the morning." The waitress slid a cup of coffee in front of Jake, and he smiled his thanks.

"That's just it. . .she might act like she's better in the morning, but the way this thing is brewing, I have a feeling it's not the end of it." Liann's forehead wrinkled.

"Maybe I should cancel going to Kansas Tech." He'd do it for Maddie, if she really needed him here. And it sounded like she did. "It's a simple two-night trip, and I'd be back before the next game, but. . ."

"It's your call. I know you aren't the only support system Maddie has. There's Billy and Justine, plus Herb and Azalea." She frowned. "I thought you'd like to know, and I didn't want it to wait. You're her guardian, and I take your role in her life as such very seriously."

"Would you meet up with all your students' parents or guardians at the Koffee Kup after eleven o'clock at night?"

"No." At this, a flush crept into her cheeks. "I probably wouldn't. I care about all my students. But Maddie's special. Um. . .you're special. But you know that."

He reached for her hand. "Please don't pull away. I want *something* to work out for us. But I don't want you to feel like you're giving up something for me. Not like ole what's-his-name. I still don't know what's going to happen with Kansas."

"I'm not sure either. The band director told me tonight that she got a call for a reference for me from Ventura High. A friend of mine said they might need a cheer coach in January, so last weekend I applied. I know it's only September and I've barely been here two months, but it's an opportunity." Liann looked down at their coffee cups and their clasped hands.

His deflated mood surprised him as he released her hand. "You should go, if they call you for an interview. See if that's the life for you still. You'll be closer to your family. And maybe ole what's-his-name will have gotten a clue."

At this, Liann smiled. "Maybe. And you're right. If I get that call from California, I'm going to go."

twelve

"Jake Tucker, welcome to Kansas!" Mike Higgins enveloped Jake in a strong hug, pounding his back. "Good to have you up here."

Higgins and Jake ran the ball during their years at Texas State. Higgins did more defensive blocking and sacking quarterbacks while Jake ran for the ball. "I've always got your back," Higgins would say.

"Thanks, man." Jake looked past Mike at the athletic complex of glass and steel. He definitely wasn't in Starlight, Texas, anymore. "Wow, what a facility."

"It's the big time." Mike had always been the size of a Mack truck. He still wore his physique well, even though his own gridiron days were long gone. "I was praying for you, man, that you'd get the chance you've always wanted. So how's life in Podunk, Texas?"

"Starlight, Mike. Starlight."

"Right. So how's your record? I know our guy flew down there to see you and y'all lost that opening game, but he liked what he saw anyway." His friend led him into the building. Activity pulsed inside. Jake could practically inhale the adrenaline flowing through the halls.

"We're two and one now. Lost to Cove, which you knew about already, but we won against Waco West and Fisher Ridge." He wondered when he'd wake up at the ranch and be smacking the snooze button. But nope, he was here for real.

"Well, I told them you'd make a solid contribution to the team here and were looking to advance." Mike paused at a display case of awards. Kansas Tech had taken the title in their division four out of the past five years.

What Jake could learn, just being an assistant on the coaching staff. The position was similar to what he did at Starlight but miles above it in status. "That's true."

Mike led him into the offices, where he met a blur of faces and a list of names. He did remember the head coach's name. Coach Rather.

"Good to meet you, Mr. Tucker." The older gentleman had a firm handshake. "I come from a small-town background myself. But one thing I believe: a field's a field. Good coaching and good playing are important at any level."

By the end of the afternoon, Jake's brain was leaking with all the facts he'd picked up about Kansas Tech. He even saw where his desk might be and met the coach he might be replacing.

That evening before sunset, he drove through the college town, looking at possible places to live. The idea of moving here alone made him look at apartments. However, he drifted into some neighborhoods with homes. He couldn't remember the last time he'd lived in a place where the homes were so close together. He didn't know how Billy slept at night, knowing that he had neighbors within a stone's throw at his and Justine's home up on the ridge in town. He'd adapted. So could Jake, he supposed.

He could picture himself in a house, too, with a big front yard. With Liann standing on the steps beside him, even. But he couldn't ask her to come here. He didn't want to even hint at pressuring her. Then again, she might be heading to

California, so Kansas would be out of the question for her anyway.

Jake drove until he found the Kansas Tech campus again and found a visitors parking spot not far from the campus park. The large lawn in front of the commons had winding brick paths, benches, and a large fountain in the center. He smelled food cooking, an aroma drifting from a dining hall somewhere.

A few students clustered around the lawn, taking advantage of the remaining daylight and the cooler temperatures. Some boys were tossing a football around, laughing and hooting when they fumbled, cheering when they caught the ball. Now, those were the days.

Jake found an empty bench and sat down, stretching his legs. He leaned his head back to look for the first stars of the night and a sliver of moon. He could bow his head to pray, but when alone outside like this, he liked to look up.

"Lord, here I am. I'm thankful for this opportunity. I know every opportunity doesn't mean a guaranteed yes from You. I don't attempt to know exactly how You work. But I'm here. You see what I've done in the past. For Dad, Billy, and now for Maddie. I want my turn, Lord. I'm tired of being the strong one, the responsible one.

"I've always wanted to make a difference in the lives of young people. There are young men who don't have a father like I did, who don't see hope for their future. They don't have someone to teach them the value of self-discipline and how to work as a team. But I can do that. I would love to work here. You know that. So please, if this is my chance or if there's something else, make the way clear for me. Amen."

Yes, he was tired of being strong and responsible. He wanted to go do something reckless and let someone else take care of the duties for a change. He didn't know what the answer would be about Kansas, or how it would come. He did know enough about the nature of God that there'd be an answer. Like any good father, the Lord would be there for him.

Call Dad.

Jake checked his phone. Colorado was an hour behind them, but it was Wednesday evening, and his parents would likely be at Bible study. Maybe he'd call in the morning. Christmas in Colorado couldn't come soon enough, to see them again face-to-face for real and not via a computer.

He almost decided to call Liann. It wouldn't be fair, he reminded himself as he thought back to the day he kissed her at the river. As she would say, "So not fair." He smiled at the thought of her face as she scolded him. The painful memory followed him back to his hotel room.

As he unlocked the door, his phone chimed with a message from Coach Blann. "Crisis. Call me ASAP. Rollins canceled his plans for TSU."

❧

"Here, you crank for a while. I'm getting old, and it hurts my shoulder." Aunt Chin Mae waved Liann over to the honey extractor sitting on top of a low table. "This might be all our honey this year. No more until spring. But we'll see."

"Oh, you're not getting old." Liann took her place in front of the extractor. She glanced into the top of the cylinder, as tall and wide as the yellow drink cooler they used during football games and band practice. Six hive frames spun on the inside, the motion drawing the honey out of the frames and into the holding tank at the bottom, where it filtered out the remaining wax particles in the honey.

Her aunt started dispensing the filtered honey into glass jars. "We finish this hive box and start the last one. Then that's all for today." She wiped her forehead with the back of her hand. "Those boxes are heavy."

"I'm glad you didn't try to lift them yourself. Forty pounds is a lot." As it was, they'd had to load several boxes onto one cart and wheel the cart over to the covered pavilion where Aunt Chin Mae worked on her honey.

Liann grabbed the crank and turned it, as if she were operating an old-fashioned ice-cream maker. Ten frames in one box and four pounds of honey per frame meant forty pounds of honey. Even with the summer drought, her aunt was proud of the bees' production.

"I have enough jars to take to the last farmers' market of the season." Aunt Chin Mae beamed. "My bees did so well this year."

The extractor's spinning interior ground to a halt. Liann lifted the clear cover to get a better look at the frames inside. She definitely identified with the spinning motion. The girls on the color guard team had changed since the night of the Homecoming dance. Before, they would laugh and talk in front of her. Now, they did their practices but kept their chatter away from her.

Maybe it was best. Perhaps a few of them were upset or jealous over her friendship with Maddie's family. If she were on the outside looking in, she'd tell herself to back off and keep a safe emotional distance. But truthfully, if any of her other girls seemed like they were struggling, she'd be there for them, too. Kristen was having trouble with precalculus and was in danger of being ineligible to participate in the upcoming marching band competitions. Liann had made a phone call and helped her enroll in free after-school tutoring two days a week.

No word from Jake, but he'd arrive home this afternoon from his Kansas trip. How he'd glowed at the idea of being invited for an interview and a visit at Kansas Tech. She prayed for him, that he'd find the answers he was looking for, just as she did for herself. Maddie had been on a tight leash with Jake gone, staying with Azalea and Herb Bush. The couple's names made her smile.

"Azalea will be here soon," Aunt Chin Mae said. "I told her to come get honey. It's good for their allergies. They get four jars a year."

"I've heard of honey helping with allergies." She wasn't a big fan of it herself but couldn't help sneaking a stray drop of sweetness as she lifted the empty frames from the extractor. She took a deep breath. The cool breeze and longer shadows promised that fall was inching ever closer.

Azalea's SUV came rumbling up the driveway, bouncing and bucking on the uneven dirt. It had rained two nights ago, so no more dust clouded around the vehicle. The vehicle came within inches of a column that supported the pavilion beside the garage.

"Good. You're here, too." Azalea looked at Liann as she slammed the door. "We've got us a real pickle brewing, a real pickle."

"What's wrong?" Liann and her aunt chorused.

"Maddie. That girl." Azalea shook her head. "I don't know but she's fryin' eggs when she says she's scramblin' them."

"Huh?" Liann blinked at Azalea.

"She's up to something, even though she's been telling me for three days everything's fine. She's been real quiet, when most other times I can't get her to find the OFF button and give us a little silence. Not that I mind. I do the same thing." Azalea patted her flaming 'do. "Soon as I got out of the salon today, picked her up from her friend Kristen's house where they were studyin', I dropped her by her own house."

"Did you get to talk to Jake?"

"I tried, but he looked awfully upset himself." Azalea shook her head. "I tell you, Chin, I'd like to take some young people today and knock their heads together. Present company excluded, Liann."

"Liann's close to the family. Aren't you?" Aunt Chin Mae patted Liann's arm. "You're so good to help them. God sent you here for them, and for you."

"I'll see what I can do. But you all have been here longer and know them better. Or maybe the pastor can help them." Liann didn't want to sound like she was making excuses, but here she'd been trying to give herself a breather, and she still wound up wanting to help them. Plus, the very mention of Jake made her think again of how much she'd missed him.

"That's all true," said Azalea. "But you have a kind heart, and you have the time and opportunity to be there for Maddie. We're all old. Justine, bless her heart, is so busy flyin' back and forth for her TV show that you're the easy choice. Plus, everyone knows how well you and Jake get along."

"I—I might be leaving after Christmas." Liann braced herself for their response.

"No—where?" Aunt Chin Mae covered her mouth with her hands. "You didn't tell me."

"I don't know for sure. I might be getting an interview, back in California. There's a position opening up that I'm qualified for." She sounded as if she were making an excuse for leaving.

"No, it's wrong. You belong here, in Starlight. I know it, I feel it." Her aunt cast a glance at Azalea. "We need to knock her head now."

"I'm. . . I'm going to at least check out the possibility at this other school." She held up her hands.

"Let me get your honey for you, Azalea." Aunt Chin Mae screwed the caps on the jars of honey she'd topped off earlier. "Here. I'm so upset, I don't know where the labels are."

"Aw, Aunt Chin Mae." Liann sighed.

"Y'all are going to have to work it out." Azalea picked up the jars. "You got a bag?"

"I'll go get an empty Walmart bag." Aunt Chin Mae stomped to the house.

≈

Liann stayed in her garage apartment that evening without coming down to supper. Her aunt was proficient in the silent treatment, as Liann had witnessed before when she got mad at Uncle Bert for some sort of transgression, usually minor.

She checked her e-mail. An invitation for an interview in Ventura. Except the representative would be in Dallas the following weekend, and could Ms. Rivers meet her there at the Hyatt and have lunch? Maybe this was the answer she'd been hoping for. And even better, she wouldn't have to miss work or a game. She replied to the invitation, accepting the interview.

For the first time in months, she logged on to Facebook. When she'd left California in July, she'd assured her friends they'd keep in touch that way. However, her schedule for her half-time job had devoured her time. She typed in her status: "Enjoying Texas, but other possibilities are on the horizon." Then she erased it before clicking ENTER.

The band director had mentioned the school district having a Facebook page, so Liann typed in "Starlight Independent School District." The page popped up. Liann started reading the district updates. Recent game scores for the sports teams, a notice to parents that report cards had been sent home, photos from students recognized for the History Club awards.

Maddie had mentioned something about Facebook once, so Liann typed in her name. Madelynn Tucker's page popped up, with a photo of her in her Homecoming dress as her profile photo. Then she read some of the postings on her page:

Madelynn Tucker: I'm so tired of all this mess. Wish it would end. Thursday 6:30 p.m.

Tonight.
Friends commented below her statement:

Love u girl! and *What's wrong? Txt me.*

The last comment made Liann freeze, from a Lashaunda Sanchez:

Well, you started it—

Feeling like a snoop, Liann clicked on Lashaunda's profile page. Lashaunda attended Starlight High and was a senior on the cheerleading squad. What did Maddie start? What was she tired of? Azalea was right, and despite Liann's resolve to stay back, she'd just walked into the middle of it again.

thirteen

Jake fumed the entire time during his five-mile run. The shadows stretched long across the road as he headed for home. The five miles hadn't helped erase the feelings that dogged him all the way back from Kansas.

Tim Rollins, turning down his TSU deal. This was his chance, his ticket, literally, away, with a once-in-a-lifetime opportunity. He would definitely talk to Tim during the school day, unless Blann had already summoned the kid to his office.

Then there was Maddie, who didn't seem happy to see him. She holed herself up in her room after Aunt Zalea dropped her off. The older woman looked like she wanted to tell him something, but with Maddie around, she didn't. Jake should have asked Maddie to leave the room while they talked. However, that would have resulted in Maddie getting upset, saying she didn't need to be treated like a child.

Call Dad.

The thought almost made him stop in midstride. That's right. He'd forgotten during the rest of his visit in Kansas, then tonight with Moody Maddie having taken up residence at Tucker Ranch. Jake quickened his steps to get home.

When he entered the house, music pounded from Maddie's room. He banged on the door. "Maddie, what in the world?"

She yanked open the door. "Uh, sorry."

"Where'd you get that CD? Did you clear it through me?"

Maddie huffed. "No, I didn't. A friend burned it for me." She stood and waited, as if giving him a cue to leave.

"Could I have it, please?" Jake refused to budge but took up the doorway.

"All right." She marched over to her CD player and yanked out the CD. "Here."

"Thank you."

Maddie stood in a face-off. "I'm talking to Dad tonight."

"Okay. Tell him I said hi, and I'll call him. I've got homework I need to finish first, though."

Jake backed away from the door. Who was this young woman? Definitely not Madelynn Tucker.

He went to the barn, where it was quiet. Plus, Maddie couldn't sneak up on him. Jake leaned on the door frame and looked out at the twilight as he waited for the phone to ring. His father answered after the first ring.

"Son, I was just thinking about you."

Already Jake felt better. "Dad, I meant to call you the other night."

"What's wrong?"

"I don't know. It's Maddie. There's something going on with a boy at school. She won't talk to me about it, not even Justine or her coach, Ms. Rivers."

"Ah, yes. Ms. Rivers. Maddie did fill us in about her awhile back."

"She did? What'd she say?"

"What a terrific woman she is. She said, 'You can tell she really loves God and loves people. She's one of the best teachers I've ever had.' That, and she doesn't give up on people. And, how you two have a, shall we say, *special* friendship."

"I guess you could call it that. Maddie's right."

"We can get back to your Ms. Rivers another time, though. I thought something sounded different with Maddie, but I couldn't tell for sure. Do we need to come down? Because we can. If it's a bigger issue than that, maybe we should have Maddie move up here with us."

"I didn't want to fail you, Dad. I've tried so hard to protect her, but right now, I don't know if what I'm doing is right or wrong sometimes." Jake sighed.

"I know. That's part of being a parent. But you haven't failed, son. You've given a lot for this family. Don't think I don't know it. Do you think a father likes the idea of leaving his children behind because of his health? Sometimes, I feel like I failed you."

"Not at all, Dad. Should I talk to Pastor? Maybe if you came one weekend, we could all talk together?"

"That sounds like a good plan. And don't tell Maddie. Your mother and I want it to be a surprise." His father's voice sounded warm. "Now, let's talk about your interview and this Ms. Rivers I've been hearing so much about—from everyone except you."

"The interview went great. Mike said they'll get back with me. And Liann? She's amazing. Right now, though, with her job situation and mine, neither one of us knows where we'll end up. She might be going back to California."

"Did you ask her about going to Kansas with you?"

"Dad, we've known each other less than three months."

"But from what I hear you've spent quality time together, and not doing superficial things like many couples do."

"Maybe, but she's recently been engaged and is afraid of committing again, especially this soon. I don't blame her."

"You sound like you're looking for a reason for you two not to be together."

"No. Not really. I just don't want to push or pull her into something that she doesn't want with all her heart. The last guy plowed her over and acted like he knew what was best for her. So, I don't want to do that. You know I get kind of opinionated."

"You don't say." His father's laugh was rich and warm. "Son, it's good to talk with you like this. I know you're a grown man and haven't needed me for many years, but you're still my boy."

"Thanks, Dad. I know." His throat swelled.

"Don't ever think you can't bring things to me."

"I won't. I'm sorry I didn't call you sooner about Maddie. Honestly, Liann saw things happening before I did." The admission stung his pride.

"Don't be too hard on yourself. Your mother and I will be there as soon as we can, and we'll see if we can figure out what's going on."

Jake ended the call. The night had fallen at last, the air cooling off the heat of the day. He'd talked to his father, and he knew everything was going to be all right. How many times did he *not* bring things to his heavenly Father as well, thinking he could handle them? Not that God wanted him to be a wimp, unable to make wise decisions. Of course God wanted His children to be mature, clear-thinking. But it was so easy for him to charge ahead with his own ideas.

His phone lit up with a text message: WELCOME BACK. MISSED U. —LIANN.

He wrote back: MISSED U 2.

❧

Tim Rollins sat across from Jake in his office on Friday

morning. He wore a scowl as if he'd been summoned to the principal's office.

"Tim, you're not in trouble."

"Then why does it feel like I am?" Tim stared at Jake's awards shelf then at the floor. "I'm not going to TSU. I changed my mind."

"Why, Tim? You're looking at a full-ride scholarship. There are hundreds of kids in this school who would appreciate a chance like this." Jake took a sip of his coffee.

"I appreciate it, Coach. I've just decided. . . I'm not going to college."

Jake shook his head. "I don't understand. You are a talented young man, and God's given you so much potential and blessed you with opportunities."

"I know. But I can't go to TSU." Tim's eyes appeared to fill with tears, and he pinched the bridge of his nose. "God can't change that."

"Don't say that, Tim. You have the chance, right in front of you."

"Why do you care?" Tim spat the words out. "You're in such a hurry to get out of here, going to the big time. You're deserting us."

Jake held back a sigh. He rubbed his forehead. "It's been my dream and my goal to one day coach college football since I was your age, maybe younger. Besides, you won't be here next year."

"Lucky you, Coach. It looks like you'll get the position." The young man frowned. "I'll never get out of here, just like my father. I've got to accept that."

Jake couldn't understand why Tim was refusing his chance for TSU. If he could hang on until spring. . . "Is it your grades? I thought they were excellent."

"My grades are fine." Tim stood, rubbing his palms on his jeans. "Coach, good luck in Kansas. I'm happy for you." He turned and left the office.

&

The buses pulled up in front of Starlight High, and Liann lined the girls up with the equipment. "Okay, ladies, let's get everything loaded up. Where's Maddie?"

"I think she's in the bathroom," Kristen said, picking up a trio of flags. "She's changing into her uniform. She put her skirt on inside out the first time."

"Good thing she's fixing it now. We won't have time once we get to Waco." Liann headed up to the first yellow bus. Jessica stood at the top of the steps by the driver.

"Hey, Ms. Rivers." The driver nodded to her. "We have room for five of you plus equipment, and the others will have to ride in the second bus. Sorry. I know y'all like to sit together."

"Don't worry. We'll manage." Liann looked at Kristen and one of the other girls. "You two, go ahead to the other bus. I'll send Maddie to sit with you." She glanced back at the gymnasium.

"Okay." Kristen and the other girl, Shaina, headed for the other bus, where band members milled outside the door.

Liann looked at the rest of the troupe. "Ladies, go ahead and board. I'm going to see where Maddie is. We're leaving in five minutes."

She hopped back onto the curb and trotted into the gym. A pair of band students, one tall, one short, wheeled a kettle drum toward the exit. "Hey, do you two know Maddie Tucker?"

"Yup, we know her." The short kid had freckles competing with acne on his face.

"Have you seen her?" Liann asked.

"Yeah, she already went out to the buses," the tall kid said. "She was in a big hurry, afraid we'd left already."

"Okay, thanks." Liann hurried back outside. They had a sixty-minute trip to Waco then a quick supper break before going right into warm-ups, before hitting the stands in time to see the kick-off.

"You ready?" Jessica asked as Liann stepped onto the bus.

"Yup. Ready to go." She didn't like them splitting up on separate buses, but it couldn't be helped. Sometimes, it happened. She found an empty seat and settled down with her MP3 player to tune out the roar and chatter of the kids.

Tonight, she wanted to see Jake. Last night she'd told him about what she'd seen on Facebook, which he verified and read more while she was on the phone with him. She was relieved that Mr. and Mrs. Tucker were arriving on Sunday. Relieved, and wondering what they'd think of her. But getting to the bottom of what was happening to Maddie—that mattered the most.

They headed north out of Starlight for Waco, down a two-lane highway flanked by ranch land. She watched the fields roll by, the cedar-covered buttes rising up from the pasture land. She tried to picture California. One of the first things she'd do after returning would be to drive to the Pacific, wiggle her toes in the sand, and wade in the surf. The nearest beach from here—as in a real Gulf Coast beach—lay about four hours southeast.

She dozed, dreaming of sand and surf and calling out cheers. She woke to feel the bus jolting to a stop. The stuffy air felt thick as oatmeal. She stood and opened the window above her head.

"Yeah! We're here, we made it!" A few of the kids cheered. Liann wanted to add her own cheers to the mix. She thought of Jake, riding along with the coaching staff and the team in their air-conditioned travel buses. The inequality of the band and color guard riding in regular school buses while the glory of the high school rode in comfort wasn't lost on Liann. She wouldn't miss that bit of Texas culture when she returned to California.

Liann climbed down with the rest of the band and stretched her tight muscles. Another thing she wouldn't miss about Texas was the road trips between schools. She waited to see her girls on her bus as they exited one by one.

"Let's get the equipment together and gather to the side." She drew back, motioning to the girls. Here came Kristen and Shaina from the other bus. No Maddie.

"Where's Maddie?" She glanced from Kristen to Shaina. "Did she get on the bus?"

"I—I didn't see her." Kristen hugged the flags she carried. "I'm sure she got on one of the buses."

"We only had two buses for the band and guard." Liann's heart started a jackhammer beat. "Captain and co-captain, get everyone organized, and I'll be right back." She ran to the second bus, emptying its last few students.

One of the drum majors stood by the door as Liann pounded up the steps and onto the bus. "Is anyone left in here?" Silly question. No dark shapes had moved in the windows. She stood and looked to the rear of the bus. Empty.

Liann flew off that bus then back to the one she rode on. She hadn't seen Maddie there, either. Her hands shook as she

reached for her cell phone and dialed. "Jake, pick up, please."
He had a million things to do right now, but he needed to
know Maddie was missing.

"Liann, I can't talk right now. I'm sorry."

"I know. But Maddie—she's missing."

"Where are you?"

"I'm by the band buses. She never got on either bus.
Someone told me she did, and our group got split up. It's
happened before, so I didn't think it was a big deal, and—"

"I'll meet you right there."

ॐ

Jake checked in with Blann. "Coach—I need to take care of
a situation. It's my sister. I'll be right back, in time for our
procession."

"Do what you've got to do, Tucker. We don't need any
more situations today. We've had enough with Tim's monkey
business in turning down TSU." Blann's tone was crusty, but
Jake heard the warmth underneath.

He started walking toward the band buses then broke
into a run. This couldn't be a coincidence. He found Liann,
fighting back tears and talking to the band director.

"Section leaders," she called to the students. "Listen up. We
need to find Maddie Tucker. She was on one of the buses,
and somehow she's not with the group."

"We saw her leaving the gym," said two of the percussion
players.

"We believe you," the band director said. "But we need to
find out if anyone remembers seeing Maddie on either one of
the buses."

Jake stepped up to them. "How did this happen?"

"We don't know, Jake." Liann's voice shook. "We were

loading the buses, and someone told me she was in the restroom. So I loaded up the others and went back to check for her."

He glanced at the band director then took Liann by the arm. "C'mon, I need to tell you something."

When they turned away from the group, her tears flowed, and each one cut him like a knife. "Jake. I never thought this would happen. Where could she be?"

"I have a suspicion." He pulled her around behind the last bus, blocking the view of the band group. "Tim Rollins left campus today. We talked to his parents, and they assumed he was still at school. I think he and Maddie made some kind of plan."

"I should have looked harder for her. I probably just missed her. Why would she do that? Why does she fight against those who love her and want to help her?" Liann gave a little sob.

Jake pulled her close, and she leaned on him. "Shhh. . . You did the right thing. And you trusted Maddie, so you didn't know she wouldn't be where she was supposed to be. We all trusted her." He sighed and closed his eyes. "I need to call the police."

Liann stood up straight. "Or maybe I should. I'm not sure what the school's protocol is, but the sooner we get people looking for her—or them—the better."

"I need to let Coach Blann know, too. He's the school's athletic program director, so technically he's acting administration this evening."

He'd failed. The realization nearly knocked him over as Liann dialed the Starlight Police Department and reported Maddie as missing. "I have her brother right here with me, ma'am," she was saying to the dispatcher. "Okay, here he is." Jake gave the information the dispatcher requested. "Except I don't know what she was wearing. I don't remember. She probably has a blue backpack with her." He also gave Tim's information. When he ended the call, Liann was wiping away fresh tears.

"I know she and Tim were together, but why this drastic move? He's got a wonderful future ahead of him at TSU, and it wouldn't surprise me if that's where Maddie decides to apply after this school year." Liann shook her head.

"Because of Cassandra Waters."

"What does she have to do with it?"

Jake frowned and looked across at the parking lot. "Everything. Because everything's changed. Rumor has it that Cassandra is pregnant."

fourteen

"Oh no." Liann's mind replayed the memories of Home-coming, of seeing Cassandra, then Tim and Maddie's argument, then Cassandra's venomous look at Maddie.

"I need to call my parents. They were planning to start driving to Texas first thing in the morning. But I can book them plane tickets instead." Jake moved one arm from around her then reached into his pocket.

"I want to go look for her." She didn't want to leave the circle of his arm. "I can go with you."

Jake shook his head. "You stay here. The rest of your girls need you. Maddie's my family, and I can go."

"I understand. But please, please call me if you hear anything."

"I will." He kissed her on the forehead before he left.

Liann regained her composure then stepped out from behind the bus. The girls from the guard clustered around the equipment. She took a deep breath as she approached.

"Okay, ladies. Maddie's not here, but we'll keep going. You're going to do a great job tonight." She saw the questioning glances. "Do any of you know if Maddie had plans to meet anyone after school, or right before last period? It's important, because she should have been on the bus today."

Most of them murmured, "No," or "She didn't say anything to me."

Kristen frowned, her dark straight hair falling around her face.

"Kristen. . . Did she say anything to you?"

"Not. . .not really. I knew she wasn't happy. She really likes Tim, but Cassandra Waters and her fellow harpies were being terrible to her because of him. Sorry, but Tim and her were over right after school got out last year." Kristin brushed her hair away from her face.

"I know most of that, but thanks for telling me." Liann stepped closer. "Hey, people are looking for her right now, and I'm sure they'll find her. We're going to go out there tonight, and we're going to do a beautiful job."

By the time they took their seats on the bleachers, the girls talked and chatted almost like they normally did, with a few glances toward Liann.

"Ms. Rivers," a young woman's voice called. Liann searched for the voice's owner and saw one of the football trainers waving at her. "Coach Blann wants to see you."

If they'd found Maddie or Tim already, Jake would have called. But for the head coach and school athletic director to be asking for her? She'd only been to the principal's office once when she was in school. That same feeling had burned itself into her memory and resurfaced now. She kept her knees from shaking as she stepped carefully along the bleachers and met the trainer at the aisle.

"Okay, let's go." She followed the young woman wearing the screaming yellow shirt and black pants, with her hair tied back in a ponytail.

The electric atmosphere of Friday night football tingled and popped in the stadium, but Liann's nerves were numb. *Lord, protect Maddie. Give her family comfort and peace. Help*

someone find her. And while You're at it, I have the feeling that
something's looming ahead for me.

The trainer led her to the door to the visitors' locker room. "Wait here, Ms. Rivers."

Seconds later, Coach Blann emerged. Gray hair, a military haircut, wire-rimmed glasses, and a shrewd gaze. His athletic physique preserved, but for a bit of a potbelly. He carried something pinched between his fingers. A toothpick?

"Ms. Rivers, we've got a serious situation here with one of your students tonight."

"Yes, Coach. As soon as I knew Maddie Tucker was missing, I let Jake know. He said he would tell you before he left, and we called the police together."

"I should've made the phone call, if we should have made a phone call at all." His words felt like a slap. "I'm the highest-ranking administrator here at this school function, and I should have been in the loop at the very beginning."

"Sir, I wasn't entirely sure of protocol, and Jake was worried about his sister. We weren't trying to go behind your back. We did think it was important for someone to be searching for her as soon as possible."

"Now because of one of *your* students, I have an outstanding player who's throwing away his future by his actions."

Liann's face grew hot, and she tried not to grit her teeth. "Coach, I think his actions a few months ago helped form his future. Also, since you're the senior administrator, Maddie Tucker is your student, too. In fact, if she hadn't joined color guard this year, you and I wouldn't be having this conversation." Her boldness made her stand up straighter.

"I'm sure this is all a simple misunderstanding, and Maddie will turn up—at home, probably. Calling the police is jumping the gun. We need to call everyone before calling the police." He lifted up a toothpick and chewed the end of it.

Unbelievable. "I care about my students, sir. When they're not where they're supposed to be and their family doesn't know where they are, I'm concerned. It was Coach Tucker's decision to search for his sister. Not mine." Even with her knees locked, they still threatened to shake.

"Coach, we're ready!" someone shouted from inside the locker room.

"You're right, it was Tucker's decision. This isn't the end of the matter, you can be sure. Keep me posted on the efforts to find her." He chomped on his toothpick for emphasis before turning his back on her and heading into the locker room.

Liann was shaking as she returned to the bleachers. She had the lowliest of positions. She still wasn't sure what violation she'd committed, if any. She couldn't call Jake about this, not when Maddie was still missing. His sister was his most important priority.

ə

Jake finally arrived at The Pit after finding someone at the game who would drive him back to Starlight for fifty dollars. The driver disappeared into the darkness. Billy and Justine's truck was in the parking lot, as were a number of familiar vehicles.

"I'm here. Have you found her yet?" Jake asked as he entered the restaurant. Tamarind had pushed four tables together to make one long table in the center of the dining room. Billy stood at the head.

"Hey, bro." Billy looked older than his twenty-nine years. "We started looking around town as soon as we heard."

Justine clutched her husband's hand, her eyes filled with tears.

"Billy called us right away," said Herb Bush. "Azalea is rounding up her ladies Bible study group to help search."

"Maddie may or may not be with Tim Rollins," Jake said. "He drives a blue Chevrolet. He left school today after first period, and his parents don't know where he is."

Billy unfolded a map of Starlight and central Texas. "If they've been gone for almost two hours, they are probably as far as Hillsboro to the north, just shy of San Antonio to the south, College Station to the East, and San Saba to the west." He used a compass to draw a circle two hours by vehicle from Starlight. "It's getting late, and some of you may not want to start driving with the head start they have. However, on the odd chance that they may have stopped, keep an eye out for his car."

"Did you try calling the Rollins family again?" Jake looked down at the map. Good thing they'd searched through town, but every minute took the kids farther from Starlight, if they'd decided to hit the road.

"Tim's dad is at the VFW. He hasn't seen him since last night and didn't seem concerned." Billy shook his head. "Said his son is seventeen and old enough to know when to come home."

"What about his mother?" Jake gritted his teeth at Mr. Rollins's casual attitude regarding his son.

"Mr. Rollins said his wife is in Dallas on business and hasn't heard from Tim." His brother rubbed his chin. "The rest of the kids are all at home, and none of them knew anything when I called."

"The police are distributing Maddie's and Tim's photos

and a description of the car, but they're not actively looking for them. They're considering it a school district matter at the moment. If anything, Maddie could get in trouble for truancy if she left before the final bell, as will Tim." Jake pulled up a chair. "If the police happen to see the kids, they'll notify us."

"I've brewed a bunch of coffee, y'all." Tamarind stood between them. "On the house. I've got covered cups, plus all the sugar and creamer anyone needs so you can take it on the road." The door opened, and in came Aunt Azalea, along with Chin Mae and Bert Rivers, and even Trudy from the Chamber of Commerce.

"If a Tucker's in trouble, we're here, everybody," Aunt Azalea announced. "Tell us what to do and where to go."

Words failed Jake, and he looked to Billy, who started assigning routes to the teams. It was better than sitting home and doing nothing. He'd talked to Mom and Dad on the way here, and booked them the first available flights into Killeen tomorrow. All the while and even now, he couldn't help but think he should have known, should have prevented this somehow. Leaving Waco with the memory of Liann's teary eyes didn't help him, either.

"Let's all pray before we head out," said Herb. "I know that even though we don't know where that little girl is, our Lord does. So we ought to look to Him."

"That's right," someone said in the group.

They all bowed their heads. "Lord, be with us tonight as we start searching the highways and the hedges for our lost lambs, Madelynn and Tim. They've lost their way, and we ask that You help bring them home to us. Amen."

"Amen," chorused the rest of the room. In spite of his

worry, Jake almost smiled. Herb wasn't a man of many words, but he made them count.

Billy handed out a recent photograph of Maddie, the one of her in her Homecoming dress. Good thinking. Jake looked at Maddie's face, smiling at the camera. He remembered their trip to Austin, dress shopping. Liann should be here right now. It didn't seem right that she wasn't.

As he crossed The Pit's parking lot on the way to his truck, he sent Liann a quick text message: NO NEWS. STILL LOOKING. WILL KEEP U POSTED.

As soon as he hit SEND, his phone started to ring. Starlight Police Department. "Jake Tucker here." He turned on his heel and headed for the restaurant.

"Mr. Tucker, this is Sergeant Huston from the Starlight Police Department. We've received word from the Department of Public Safety that a vehicle with a male and female occupant matching the description you gave us lost control and crashed on Highway 84 just south of Abilene tonight."

fifteen

Liann cried for most of the weekend. She wasn't usually given to tears, but after what had happened on Friday night, she dared anyone to blame her for her actions. Sweet, sweet Maddie lay in an Abilene hospital with both legs fractured, along with a fractured jaw from the air bag. Liann wanted to hop in Aunt Chin Mae's Smart Car and make the trek to Abilene.

However, part of her still felt a little responsible for what had happened. She should have done more. She and Jake knew there were issues, and what they did hadn't been enough to avert disaster. Ever since Jake's call late Friday evening, she'd stayed away.

Plus, Coach Blann's words still stung. The man was protecting the hierarchy of the football team. It seemed a football player was worth more than a sweet, confused girl who'd listened to lies and let herself become lost in her search for love.

The seventeen-year-old male in the car wreck walked away with only a few bruises, she read in the Sunday newspaper. If Coach was trying to keep the news of the couple's doomed road trip quiet, he was unsuccessful. While not naming Tim by name, Starlight was small enough for people to read between the lines.

She logged on to her school district e-mail and found a message on Sunday evening, from Principal Peterson:

Please come to my office at 7 a.m. on Monday.

Great. Coach Blann had said something about this not being the end of the matter.

A knock sounded on the apartment door. "Hello, Liann. You need to come eat something. I. . .I cooked steak," said Aunt Chin Mae. "Real steak. Not steak in a box."

Liann sat up straight on the couch. Aunt Chin Mae, cooking? As in not-heating-up-a-frozen-dinner cooking? "Oh, you didn't have to." She rose and crossed the room, opening the door.

Aunt Chin Mae's face brightened. "You come down. Please. You shouldn't suffer alone. You did the best you could. It was not your fault." Her aunt tugged on her arm. "Besides, someone's here to see you."

"Who?"

"You need to come downstairs and see." Aunt Chin Mae tugged on her arm until Liann followed.

Jake's truck was in the driveway, and he stood at the bottom of the stairs outside the garage. "I was hoping she could get you to come down."

She tried not to rush down the stairs and knock her aunt over, but Aunt Chin Mae sidestepped just in time. "Jake!" She flew into his arms.

He held her tightly, and she almost couldn't breathe for a moment. "I would've come sooner," he said in her ear.

"I know. How's Maddie? Why are you here, in Starlight?"

"I have to work tomorrow, same as you. My parents are in Abilene with Maddie. Once she's well enough to travel, they're moving her to Colorado. No arguments." He looked as if he'd shed a burden. "I didn't realize how hard it was, how

I was taking on more than I should have."

"Me either." She realized he still had his arms around her, and she didn't care. "Why did she and Tim run off like that?"

Jake planted a kiss on the top of her head before releasing her. "Maddie decided she wanted to be in Colorado, and Tim was taking her. His last hurrah, of sorts, before owning up to the fact he's going to be a father."

"So it's true then, not a rumor." Liann shook her head. "Oh, these kids. Did Maddie know when she left with him?"

"She thought it was just a cruel rumor. And now, she's devastated. Tim's going to have to grow up a lot faster, have a lot bigger priorities than his studies. I'm hoping to talk him into getting some job training, at least."

Liann didn't miss the hooded expression in his eyes. "Some good kids made some really bad decisions. But we tried, Jake. We tried."

"That we did." He glanced at her more closely. "How are you doing after what happened? I've been worried about you."

She frowned. "I'm scared. Coach Blann was awful the other night. He seemed to think I overreacted about Maddie. He didn't even want the police to know right away."

Jake sighed. "He's got the old-guard, good-old-boy mentality. Ridiculous. I'll probably hear it when I go in tomorrow, but I don't care. That's my sister. I had to find her."

She nodded. "He—He's got me worried, though. He said this isn't the end of it, not for me."

"I wouldn't worry."

"That's easy for you to say. I just got an e-mail from Principal Peterson, calling me in for a meeting first thing tomorrow morning. I can't think of anything that I've done wrong." Liann looked into his eyes. "Please, if it comes down to it, stick up for me in case you get called in, too."

"I'll be there for you. But don't worry. Everything will be fine."

But Liann saw a glimmer of doubt in his eyes.

❧

"Good morning, Ms. Rivers." Jacob Peterson sat behind his massive maple desk that dwarfed the chairs in front of it. "I understand you've had quite a weekend."

"Yes, it was. About Madelynn Tucker—"

"I'll need a statement of everything you did from the time you found out she was missing. From what it sounded like at first, you knew she had left the campus but said nothing until you arrived in Waco."

"No, that's not true."

"Did you see her get on the bus?"

"No, but—"

"It's a teacher's responsibility to ensure that her students are accounted for before they leave campus for a function."

If he would just let her explain. She'd already decided she wasn't up to being at school today and was taking a personal day off. "I was told she'd gone outside and boarded a bus. We were separated. That happens sometimes."

"Additionally, I understand that Madelynn Tucker and several of your students have been harassing Cassandra Waters." He held up a stack of papers.

"No, if anything, it was probably the other way around. I saw Cassandra Waters the night of Homecoming, and she looked anything but harassed by Madelynn Tucker. And why wasn't I told about this matter concerning my students?" She was treading water but going down for the third time. She cast a glance around the office. No life preserver appeared.

"It's just recently come to my attention." The principal took a sip from the coffee cup on his desk. "You've done an outstanding job so far this year with your class. That's in your favor. But this. . .this is a serious matter, and I'm looking at it from the other side."

Liann sat up straighter. "I know. You have to look at a situation from all sides. I—I wasn't expecting Maddie to do something like this. I knew she'd been unhappy lately, but her attendance record is perfect. So what else do I need to do?"

"You need to seek counsel from the teachers' union. They can help you." Mr. Peterson sat back in his desk chair. "Like I said, you've done remarkable things with our group this year, and it would be a shame for you to be removed for disciplinary reasons. Jessica has given you shining reviews. No matter how it looks, we've got your back. You'll have a chance to tell your story."

"Thank you. I've called a sub for today, and she should be arriving at any moment." She fled from the office, her face burning. No one said anything to her, but she knew the faculty and probably all the students knew the story, or most of it anyway.

Liann entered the gymnasium and walked to the band wing where the offices were. Jessica popped out of her doorway.

"Liann." She darted a look to the side. "In case Big Brother is watching, I wanted to let you know I'm here for you. This is a bunch of bunk. Someone has an ax to grind, and you're the easy target. You're expendable, and it's not right."

"That's what Mr. Peterson said—he's going to back me up, too. But I have an interview on Saturday for Ventura. So my time here might be limited anyway." Although after

Jake showed up at the house, she knew at least one person wouldn't want her to leave. Of course, he still had his Kansas dream he was free to follow, now that Maddie would be moving to Colorado.

"Keep me posted," Jessica said as Liann left the offices.

"I will if I can." As Liann crossed the parking lot, she saw the football team out doing drills first thing. There stood Jake. He glanced in her direction then stepped around the tall chain-link fence and headed toward her.

"I'm not supposed to talk to you," he said.

She stopped at the Smart Car. "I know. Someone's blowing this way out of proportion. Someone besides Coach Blann. I don't know why, Jake. But right now, it's enough to make me want to take the first flight out of here and go. I don't need this. I didn't want to come here and stay. I didn't want to fall. . ."

Yes, she'd fallen for Jake Tucker.

"Same here."

"Stand up for me, Jake." She tried not to plead.

"I have to be careful—"

"Why? To save your own skin? To protect your position? Are you part of the 'old guard' that you were talking about?" She stepped toward him and jabbed his chest with her index finger. "Do you want to keep your prime job here in Starlight? Just in case Kansas Tech passes, you'll still have a backup plan, and the top position in Starlight would make you a very big fish in a tiny pond."

Jake stepped away from her, fists on hips. "C'mon, Liann. I wouldn't do that to you."

"By standing by and doing nothing, you're agreeing with them. With Blann." She shook her head. "Talk to the campus security. Surely they have video of people leaving. See what time Maddie left with Tim. Because there's no proof of when she left campus. Unless you can talk to her yourself."

"I'm not going to just stand by."

She wanted to scream. "You know what? Never mind. This is just a part-time job, in a little rinky-dink town. Take care, Jake."

"Liann—"

She held up one hand as she fumbled with her car keys in the other.

❧

"So Ms. Rivers isn't coming back?" Maddie sounded as though she had cotton in her mouth. She sank back into her pillows, fresh tears streaming down her cheeks. "It's all my fault. . .all my fault."

"We don't know if she's coming back." Jake stood by his sister's hospital bed on Wednesday. He'd taken a personal day to meet his parents in Abilene and visit Maddie. She needed to know what her actions—and Tim's—had cost people. Had cost him. Liann would probably never speak to him again.

"It's not fair." She hiccuped then winced. "I was going to call once we crossed into New Mexico, to tell Mom and Dad we were coming."

"Sweet pea, if you wanted to come see us, you should have called beforehand." Mom sounded tired. She sighed and looked at Dad. "Nobody was *making* you stay in Texas."

"I know. But Tim and I just wanted to. . .just go. . .and I told him about Colorado. So we started making plans to go." She frowned. "I thought Cassandra was lying about the baby. He told me it might not be his, even if she *is* pregnant."

"Tim's going to have to grow up a lot faster than he planned," Jake said.

"He hasn't called me, at all." Her voice quavered. "Guess that means. . ." She sobbed then hiccuped again. "Ouch. I was so stupid about him."

Jake opened his mouth to say something then realized he wasn't the parent here. He never had been. Not really. Both he and Liann had taken on roles for Maddie that they probably shouldn't have. Not that they shouldn't care. *Lord, forgive us. We acted out of love for her, and concern.*

Mom drew close to Maddie's bedside. "Honey, you are still loved. Very, very much." She brushed Maddie's hair back.

Dad motioned Jake into the hallway. "Son, when will we get to meet this Liann? What's going on? I realize we're hours and hours away, but I thought she might come with you."

"Dad, I don't know when. I—I don't know when I'm going to see her again. She's. . . She's planning to leave Starlight for good." The thought sliced into him, all thoughts of Kansas Tech shoved aside for the moment. "I tried to explain to her, how we have to be careful—"

"Why? Is someone in trouble over what happened to Maddie?"

"Liann."

"Over our daughter?"

"Yes, sort of." That wasn't the truth. "Yes, because of how she handled things on Friday night. That, and Coach Blann was trying to protect Tim. I think he was hoping Tim would reconsider TSU's offer."

"You can't let this travesty continue. I don't care who people think they are."

"You're right, Dad. I can't."

sixteen

Despite Aunt Chin Mae's offer of the Smart Car, Liann rented a car and drove to Dallas for her interview at the Hyatt with the Ventura recruiter. She clipped along the sidewalk in her favorite heels, saved for occasions like this. And her favorite suit with the purple blouse. She'd done her hair like she hadn't in months, her makeup perfect with smoky eyes and just enough blusher and a light lip gloss. This was a cheer coach position, something far, far different than her interview for the ragtag color guard team back in Starlight.

She met Misty Rossetti in the foyer. Funny. Maddie's horse was named Misty. This made her grin as she and Misty shook hands. This Misty wasn't old, grayish, and lumbering, though.

"Thanks for accepting my invitation to interview," Misty said, flashing gleaming white teeth. "I've reserved a small conference room here so I can show you the PowerPoint presentation about the Ventura cheer program."

"Sounds great. I'm looking forward to it."

Misty led her down a hall off the lobby and into a tiny meeting room containing a conference table with a dozen padded chairs. A laptop sat at one end of the long table, facing a blank wall. "If you'd like some water, help yourself, and we'll get started."

"Thanks. It's been quite a drive from Starlight." Liann

took a glass from the table and filled it from a pitcher. She took a seat as Misty dimmed the lights.

Music blared from the laptop's speakers as the Power-Point began. "Ventura means. . .VICTORY." Wow. That sounded like the guy who did movie preview voice-overs. *"In a world. . ."*

Faces of cheerleaders, their hair pulled back and festooned with bows, appeared on the screen. "We have a long tradition of cheer at Ventura, a spirited legacy that continues with the next generation of students to come through our halls."

Video of formations—amazing ones—played on the screen. Liann had to admit she missed the gymnastics portion of cheer—the physical skills and pyramids. The catches and flips. Music with a pounding beat accented the performances.

"Should you join us at Ventura, you will join us in bringing cheer to the next level. Higher, stronger, louder. The question is: Are you worthy?"

Liann blinked when the lights came on. No, she didn't know if she was worthy. "That was quite a presentation."

"It's brand new this year," Misty said, taking a seat across from Liann. "All right, Ms. Rivers, now that you've seen the presentation, do you have any questions?"

"So, what's your position on hazing or bullying, even among cheerleaders?"

"We have a zero tolerance policy for such behaviors." Misty blinked. She probably didn't get asked questions like that every day.

"That's great." Liann paused. A sudden realization stopped her. Ventura wasn't for her, not the cushy position, the polished glamour. She'd exchanged that dream for a new one. She belonged in Starlight. She was sorry it had taken renting a car and taking up Misty Rossetti's time, but, at least she knew. Liann stood.

Misty did as well, a questioning look on her face. "Is everything all right, Ms. Rivers?"

"Yes, it is. I just realized, Ventura's not for me." She shifted, avoiding Misty's eyes. How could she explain? "I wish you the best in finding a coach, though. Thanks for meeting with me."

"Thank you."

Liann left Misty, her mouth still gaping. By the time Liann found her rental car, her hands were shaking. What had she just done? She'd prayed last night for clarity. Oh, she'd received clarity, all right. Watching the images paraded across the screen, she realized they were just that. Images.

"Lord," she said as she started the car, "I have no idea where I'm going or what I'm doing. I know now what I'm *not* doing. That was easy today. But what's next?" She found I-35 and headed south, home to Starlight. Home? Home for now, anyway.

She turned on the radio as she zipped along the highway. Maybe she could go back to college. She'd studied education, but what she really enjoyed was helping students. Matt was half right. She did want to help young people. She could always go back to school to become a counselor or an adolescent psychologist. She still had a lot to learn. She should have kept herself at a better emotional distance from her students, for one thing. Emotions seemed to run high when she cared.

Liann thought back to Monday, how she'd given Jake a verbal lashing. He hadn't said he *wouldn't* stand up for her. All he'd said was he needed to be careful. But still, that said something. If he did love her—not that he'd ever said he loved her—he'd put his heart's desire on the line for her. This time, she wasn't going to settle for a man who loved himself and his position in life above her.

"I love you, Jake Tucker," she said aloud in the car. "The question is: How much do you love me?"

☙

"Emma Waters and her daughter are behind these ridiculous allegations," said Jake before the school board on Monday night. "I appeal to you to look at the facts of what happened— which really have nothing to do with Ms. Waters and have everything to do with Tim Rollins and my sister, Madelynn Tucker. Ms. Rivers brought concerns to me on several occasions due to conversations she'd had with Maddie, as well as my sister's Facebook page. I appreciate that. She was doing her job as a teacher who truly cares for her students, both on and off the clock. You will see that these young women who allege they were harassed were, in fact, the ones doing the harassing. Of *my* sister."

The school board was assembled in one row along with the superintendent. The president of the school board spoke. "Coach Tucker, we thank you for bringing this matter to our attention. There are a lot of facts and statements to sort through, but we will get to the bottom of it and give our ruling to the Human Resources department." She smiled at him.

"Thanks, ma'am. I won't take up any more of your time." Jake turned to see his parents, plus Aunt Zalea and Uncle Herb, plus others who were there that night when Maddie disappeared. He wished Liann had come, but she had sent word through her aunt and uncle that she thought it better not to.

He owed her an apology, he knew, but tonight he'd publicly put his job on the line and address the school board. He could probably kiss the head coaching job a long good-bye. Blann would find someone else, probably one of the egomaniac assistant coaches who would love to spend time rubbing Jake's nose in the fact that he'd thrown away the position over a woman.

Not over any woman. The woman he loved.

In his pocket, he carried a polite letter from Kansas Tech, thanking him for his interest in being part of the athletic coaching team for their institution.

Although you exhibit many fine qualities of a coach that we look for when recruiting for our staff, you have not been selected for a position at this time.

❧

Liann had spent the three days since her bombed interview for Ventura helping Aunt Chin Mae close the hives for the season. October had blown in with cooler temperatures, and mornings held a crispness in the air that energized rather than drained her.

Azalea Bush had called last night, singing Jake's praises. "Oh, darlin', it was just like David and Goliath, him in front of the school board with his five smooth stones. You just keep prayin', and we will, too."

No answers had blown in on the wind, although she had received assurances from the teachers' union that her interests were protected, and she needed to continue carrying out her teaching duties, which she'd done. She had also looked at the catalog for Texas A&M–Central Texas. The university was close enough for her to pursue more studies once she'd lived in Texas long enough to be considered a resident. However, she couldn't imagine Starlight without Jake, or her in Starlight without him.

A pair of vehicles pulled up in the driveway, one of them a large boxy van and the other, Jake's truck. Its bed brimmed with boxes tied down by bungee cords. Was he moving?

Some kind of fuss was going on beside the van as Liann approached. Maddie settled onto the seat of a wheelchair with a couple helping her. The man was an older version of Jake with touches of gray in his hair. The woman, Maddie's mother, had dark hair like her daughter, kind brown eyes, and a big smile that Maddie had inherited.

"Ms. Rivers!"

Liann ran to them. "Maddie!" She hugged the girl, who immediately began sobbing.

"I'm so sorry. I'm so sorry. All you ever did was push me to do better. You stuck up for me, and now you're in trouble. And it's all my fault." Maddie buried her face in Liann's shoulder.

"Don't cry. It's going to be okay." Liann straightened and stood to face Maddy's parents. Jake's parents. What must they think of her?

"Melvin Tucker," Jake's dad said, extending his hand. "I want to thank you for everything you've done for our Madelynn."

"I'm June Tucker," said Maddie's mom. "And I'm a hugger." With that, she enfolded Liann in a motherly embrace. The gesture made Liann miss her own mother. Liann stepped back, glancing at Jake.

"And you know me." Jake quirked a grin. "Listen, about last Monday—"

"Don't." Liann shook her head. "I was upset—really upset.

I'm sorry. I said some things I probably shouldn't have."

His voice grew soft. "I didn't want to let you down. That's the last thing I'd ever want to do."

"I think we'll go say hi to Chin Mae and Bert," June said. She grasped the handles of the wheelchair and pushed it toward the house.

Liann stood fixed where she was. If Jake was leaving, she didn't want to rake her heart over broken glass.

He stepped closer.

"So," she heard herself asking, "you heard from Kansas Tech?"

He nodded, and she felt her heart splinter. "I got a letter. They said thanks, but no thanks."

"You mean—"

"I'm staying here."

No, her heart wasn't splintering. "What about your job here in Starlight?"

"I'm still assistant coach, for now."

"You're not leaving, then?" He wasn't going, and neither was she, so that meant. . .

He shook his head. "No, this is all of Maddie's stuff. We're moving her up to Colorado to be with Mom and Dad, where she ought to be. She's been suspended for a week because of leaving campus without permission like that. Starlight ISD is putting that on her record and sending it to Colorado. We're actually leaving for Colorado now. I have some personal days I can take, and I plan to be back here in time for Friday night's game."

"I'm sure going to miss her."

"So, what about you? Are you going to Ventura?"

"No. I got all the way up there, heard their spiel, and

realized I don't want that anymore. I decided to stay here. I've grown partial to spinning flags and tossing rifles." She stepped closer to him. "I'm also looking at going to grad school, to be an adolescent counselor."

A grin slid across his face. "You're staying? Here?"

She nodded then threw her arms around his neck and kissed him, not caring if anyone happened to glance out the window. "I'm not leaving, Jake. I want to be here, with you. That's what I really want. To ride Patch and Misty, and get stranded, and go fishing, and find out more about Billy and Justine's cottages. I want to dig for fossils and harvest honey and go through the Dairy Queen drive-through. And go to Austin for some really good shoe shopping."

Jake pulled her into his arms, lifted her up, and spun her around. "I think all that can be arranged."

"Good, because I'm staying. You're stuck with me," she said as a laugh tickled her throat.

He kissed her. "Good, 'cause I'm not going anywhere either. Except to Colorado and back."

Liann frowned. "I'm going to miss you. I feel like we have lost time to make up for."

"So come with me right now. Today."

"To Colorado?"

"Of course. I could use a driver. It's a good fourteen hours probably, longer with Maddie. Mom and Dad are along, too. I know they'll enjoy getting to know you."

"I'll pack now." I'm not due back at school until Monday. Liann stepped back, but he held her hand.

"Not so fast. One more thing."

"What's that?"

"I love you, Liann Rivers. More than my job, more than

any of this." He kissed her one more time.

"I love you, too, Jake Tucker." She had come to Starlight, praying God would turn the mess she'd made into something beautiful. And so He had, for all of them.

epilogue

"Guess who's getting married?" Aunt Chin Mae marched into Liann's apartment, waving a newspaper.

"Me! That's who!" Liann felt like she'd reverted to a giggly teenager again, but when she looked at herself in the full-length mirror, she saw herself in a wedding gown. April, the perfect time for a wedding in Texas, with the bluebonnets and Indian paintbrush gracing the fields outside with riots of color.

And downstairs, outside at the beautiful view of the west from her aunt and uncle's property, rows of white chairs faced an outdoor altar underneath the ancient live oak. In less than fifteen minutes, Liann would head down the steps with her father, cross the parking lot, and walk down an aisle of fresh grass to become Mrs. Jake Tucker.

"Not just you getting married, silly." Aunt Chin Mae laughed. "Your old Matt. See?"

"I don't care," said Liann's mother. "I'm finally getting to wear my mother-of-the-bride dress today."

"Let me see." Liann reached for the paper. She'd always wondered what happened to Matt. There he was, on the society page of the *Austin American-Statesman*. Matthew LeFleur set to wed Christina McElvey on June 22nd. Ironic, almost a year to the day of what would have been their old wedding date. " 'The groom-to-be is the youth pastor at Grace Covenant Church. The bride-to-be is a physical education teacher in Austin Public Schools, as well as a piano player at Grace Covenant Church.'"

"What? Let me see that." Tamarind, wearing her bridesmaid dress in a gorgeous shade of periwinkle, leaned over her shoulder. "I knew there was something fishy about him."

Liann laughed at the irony. One of her last memories before everything caved in was Matt wanting her to learn to play piano. Ancient history. All things were now made new. She shook her head and tossed the paper back to her aunt. "Can someone get me a damp cloth? I need to get this ink off my hands." She silently wished Matt well then put him out of her mind forever.

"Right here," said Justine, removing a wipe from a package in her purse. "I'm well prepared."

Maddie crossed the apartment with only the slightest of limps. "You're so beautiful, Liann. I'm so glad I'm getting another sister." She'd healed up and blossomed during her time in Colorado and had decided to let her mother homeschool her. Tim Rollins was working and finishing his senior year, preparing to enter the work force to help support his baby boy.

"Ladies, we need some bridesmaids lined up downstairs right now," Billy called up the stairs.

"Guess that's us!" Maddie went to grab her bouquet on the table.

"Okay, mother of the bride, too," came Billy's voice again.

"That's right," Liann's mother said. "I don't want anyone to miss me in this dress." Nobody would, not with all the sequins. "C'mon, Chin Mae. You can walk behind me."

"I'm not supposed to be here. I'm supposed to be in my seat." But Aunt Chin Mae trotted after Liann's mother.

Liann was left with her four bridesmaids, Maddie, Justine,

Tamarind, and Beth. "Ladies, thank you all for every way you've added to my life since I've moved to Starlight. I once thought it was one of the worst mistakes I'd ever made, but now my life is full to overflowing."

Maddie nodded. "Plus, you'll have the best seats at the football games next fall, married to the head coach of the Starlight High Yellowjackets."

"Yes, I sure will, won't I?" A laugh bubbled up inside her at Maddie's words. "But I'm not going to wear that hideous yellow shirt anymore."

At that, the women laughed as Liann's father climbed the stairs. "Baby girl, we're ready to go now." He looked distinguished in his tuxedo, and Liann wished now that California wasn't so far away.

"Daddy, you never told me what you think of Jake." She had no doubts in her heart about him.

"You did good, Li. You did good."

With that, Liann placed her hand on her father's arm and stepped downstairs into her new life.

Author's Note

I hope you enjoyed another journey to Starlight, a sweet little town with lots going on in the heart of Texas, near Fort Hood. Starlight is a blend of all the cities and towns in the area, where in fall, high school football is king. During August, the marching bands and football teams step up their game to give their towns a season they'll never forget. Rebecca's Kitchen is a real restaurant in Kempner, Texas, that serves amazing pies and good down-home country cooking. But that's the only real character from the Fort Hood area in *Counting on Starlight*.